GIRL
IN LANDSCAPE

Jonathan Lethem is the author of six novels, the most recent being *The Fortress of Solitude* (2003). *Motherless Brooklyn* (1999) was named Novel of the Year by *Esquire* and won the National Book Critics Circle Award and the Salon Book Award. He has also written a story collection and a novella, has edited *The Vintage Book of Amnesia*, guest-edited *The Year's Best Music Writing 2002*, and was the founding fiction editor of *Fence* magazine. His writings have appeared in *The New Yorker*, *Rolling Stone*, *McSweeney's* and many other periodicals. He lives in Brooklyn, New York.

ALSO BY JONATHAN LETHEM

GIRL
IN LANDSCAPE

Jonathan Lethem

ff

faber and faber

First published in the United States in 1998
by Doubleday, a division of Random House, Inc.
1540 Broadway, New York, New York 10036

First published in the United Kingdom in 2002
by Faber and Faber Limited
3 Queen Square London WC1N 3AU

Printed in England by Mackays of Chatham plc, Chatham, Kent

This paperback edition first published in 2005

Jonathan Lethem is hereby identified as the author of this
work in accordance with Section 77 of the Copyright,
Designs and Patents Act 1988

A CIP record for this book
is available from the British Library

ISBN 0-571-22528-4

10 9 8 7 6 5 4 3 2 1

The sight of the mountains far away was sometimes so comprehensible to Natalie that she forced tears into her eyes, or lay on the grass, unable, after a point, to absorb it . . . or to turn it into more than her own capacity for containing it; she was not able to leave the fields and the mountains alone where she found them, but required herself to take them in and use them, a carrier of something simultaneously real and unreal . . .

—*Shirley Jackson*, Hangsaman

Screw ambiguity. Perversion and corruption masquerade as ambiguity. I don't trust ambiguity.

—*John Wayne*

I

BROOKLYN HEIGHTS

Clement Marsh

Caitlin Marsh

Pella Marsh (13)

Raymond Marsh (10)

David Marsh (7)

One

Mother and daughter worked together, dressing the two young boys, tucking them into their outfits. The boys slithered under their hands, delighted, impatient, eyes darting sideways. They nearly groaned with momentary pleasure. The four were going to the beach, so their bodies had to be sealed against the sun. The boys had never been there. The girl had, just once. She could barely remember.

The girl's name was Pella Marsh.

The family was moving to a distant place, an impossible place. Distance itself haunted them, the distance they had yet to go. It had infected them, invaded the space of their family. So the trip to the beach was a blind, a small expedition to cover talk of the larger one.

"They don't build arches, or *anything*, anymore," said Caitlin Marsh, speaking of the faraway place, the frontier. "Pella, help David find his shoes."

"Why are they called Archbuilders, then?" said

Raymond, the older of the two boys. He sat beside his brother on the bed. He already wore his shoes.

The boy's question was breathless, his imagination straining to reach the place the family would go. Straining to match the velocity of the coming change.

He scuffed his shoes together, waiting for an answer.

"They aren't called Archbuilders," said Caitlin Marsh. "They call *themselves* Archbuilders. What's left of them, anyway. Most of them went away."

As their mother spoke of the planet where the family would move, about the creatures there, she spun the place into existence before their eager eyes. Directing the talk at her sons, she made the journey sound like a game, her voice lyrical and persuasive.

"Went away where?" said Raymond.

"Just a minute, Ray," said Caitlin Marsh. "David needs his shoes."

But the girl knew the talk was for her sake as much as for her brothers', and she listened, intent on hearing a mistake or misunderstanding in the talk, a flat note in the song her mother was singing. Something she could point out to make it all come undone, so the family would have to stay.

"I've got one," said David, pointing to his shoe, smiling up at his mother weakly. The boys were daunted and obedient, spellbound, sensing the strangeness in their mother.

"Where's the *other* one?" said Caitlin wearily. "Pella, help him."

Caitlin's long black hair fell over her face as she

turned from the children's dresser to the closet. She was distressed, almost frantic. The girl wanted to fix her mother's hair for her, draw it back.

Draw them all back, if she could. Back some months ago, before her father had lost his election, before the idea of leaving had ever occurred to her parents. Draw herself back before her period had come. Before blood, before loss, before Archbuilders.

"They went away where?" said Raymond again.

"They went into space, far away," said Caitlin.

"But where?" said Raymond.

"Nobody knows. The ones we'll meet are the ones who stayed. There's not too many. But they're very particular about the words they pick in English. Archbuilders is how they see themselves, even if they don't build arches."

"That's kind of stupid," said Raymond thoughtfully.

"Do they have families?" said David.

"They live a long time," said Caitlin. "So they hardly ever have kids. And there aren't men and women Archbuilders. Just one kind. They're called hermaphrodites."

She was overwhelming them, piling the facts on almost nonsensically. The only thread that connected all the nonsense was Caitlin's insistence, her urgency. Her motheringness.

"What's *that?*" said Raymond.

"It's when you're a man and a woman at the same time."

"Say it again."

Caitlin repeated the word, and Raymond and David both rehearsed it, tittering.

"Here," said Pella, after digging under the bed and finding David's shoe. It was enclosed in a sort of web of dust, as though they'd already abandoned their house and come back centuries later to search for this shoe. Pella pulled the shoe out and brushed it off.

"Help him with it," said Caitlin, from the closet. She organized the beach stuff: blanket, sand toys, sun cones. "Lace his pants in so there's no skin showing. You know how."

Pella sighed, but lifted David's foot and tucked it into the shoe. Pella always touched her brothers tenderly, even when she was furious. And David, the moment he was touched, was passive, like a kitten seized by the nape.

"Thank you, Pella," said Caitlin, as she pushed a carton of old blankets back into the chaos of the children's closet, the outgrown clothes, the board games, forgotten things soon to be abandoned.

"Where do they live if they don't build anything?" said Raymond.

Pella stopped at the window. Put her fingers to the sealed layers of glass, darkened to blunt the sun. Outside was the river, the bridge. The tunnels and towers of Manhattan. The world. Don't take me away from the real world, she thought.

"They live outside, anywhere," said Caitlin.

"There's not too many of them around now. Just a few."

"Like animals?" said Raymond.

"They changed the weather," said Caitlin. "So it's always pleasant outside. There was a time before when the Archbuilders were very good at science. That was when they built arches, too. Come on, I'll tell you at the beach."

Caitlin herded them toward the basement. David began by carrying the flattened sun cones, but their circumference was bigger than he was tall, and he had to lift them over his head to keep them from scraping along the stairs. Caitlin and Raymond laughed at him, Caitlin openly, happily, her pensiveness suddenly lifted. Then she had Pella trade with David. Pella carried the cones, he took the blanket.

Pella decided not to laugh today.

Their subway car sat silent and ready in its port, its burnished shell radiant in the gloom. Raymond and David had been sneaking down to play in the brightly lit cabin of the car in the otherwise shadowy basement, and Pella could have predicted that she would find the interior littered with Raymond's action figures, hero duck and villain ducks, plastic headquarters and helicopter, fake rocks and trees. She gave an exaggerated sigh when she saw them. But Caitlin just smiled, unflappable again. She swept the toys out and loaded in the beach stuff.

They climbed in, knees nestled together in the middle of the car, cones upright against the opposite seat. Caitlin keyed in the request. It was five minutes before the network responded and black steel arms drew them out of their basement and fastened them to the passing train.

"This used to be one of the old subway lines," said Caitlin. "The F. One of the ones from before the network, when it was just a few trains, real trains that everyone rode on together. I used to take it to the beach with your grandmother and walk on the boardwalk and go to Nathan's and eat hot dogs, and you know what else they sold?"

"Frog legs, Caitlin, you already told us this story," said Raymond.

"Yick," said David.

"Shut up," said Raymond.

"It's disgusting," said David.

"Frog arms, frog heads, frog ears, frog dicks," hissed Raymond, close to David's ear.

"Stop!"

Pella nudged her brothers apart and sat between them, preempting the inevitable request from her mother. Jammed between them, she thought of the night of Clement's concession speech, the three of them seated in that ballroom, waiting, Raymond and David kicking at each other under her chair, stirring the desultory balloons that lay everywhere, decorated with Clement's name. Pella had taken one of the balloons and twisted it until it squeaked, then tore.

Clipped onto the side of the train, they roared through the black tunnel, their faces lit in bursts by the colored lights of the ads that strobed out of the darkness, eye-blink retinal tattoos. The antic iron rattle of the subway consoled Pella. She imagined she could smell the heated metal. She was in a place where she belonged, under New York City, her family in their private car a discrete unit in a teeming hive, buried out of sight of the sky. She let the pounding of the track drown her mother's words.

"The Archbuilders had a strange science. They used viruses to change things. They used viruses to build arches and a lot of other stuff, and then they changed the weather, so it was always warm and there was plenty of food around. And when they changed the weather the Archbuilders changed, too. They stopped building arches."

"Why?" said Raymond.

"The weather changed their *temperament,*" said Caitlin. "They got different priorities. Some of them went into space. And the ones who stayed forgot a lot of stuff they knew before."

"Will we live outside?" said David.

Caitlin laughed.

Pella let her brothers ask the questions. She listened to the tone of Caitlin's answers, urgent and beguiling. She could hear her mother making the idea of the family moving to the Planet of the Archbuilders real, inflating it to fill the space that had gaped when Clement lost the election.

As the train slowed at the beach station their car was unclipped and slotted into the vast parking garage under the station. Caitlin led them to the elevator. SURFACE

WARNING signs came to life as they passed up through the underground.

The doors opened to a concrete bunker, lit with blinking fluorescent, floor littered with sand, sunlight leaking from around a corner. Pella lugged out the flattened cones. Caitlin leaned her bag of sandwiches and toys against a wall, took one of the cones and unfolded it over David. Pella began to do the same with Raymond, but he snatched it away.

"I can do it myself," he said.

"Fine," said Pella. She took her own and fitted the headpiece around her skull, then let the weighted outer ring fall to the ground, tenting her inside the transparent cone.

"Mine's too big," said David. He kicked at it where it scraped the concrete.

"That's good," said Caitlin. "You won't get burned. Better than too small."

"It looks dumb."

"Nobody cares how it looks," said Pella.

"Probably there's nobody there anyway, stupid," said Raymond, his voice scornful and uncertain at once.

Raymond and David had only played in sand at a nature parlor called 'Scapes.

They walked out in their four cones toward the sunlight. Pella lifted the edge of hers and felt the concrete wall as they turned the corner. The wall was cold. It thrummed, too, with the confirming thrum that was everywhere, elevators and climate-control devices vibrant in the underground concrete and steel.

Everywhere except where they were going: outside.

"Pella," said Caitlin, and Pella let her cone fall to cover her again, felt it rasp in the grit at her feet.

They stepped out of the shade of the bunker, and the scattering of sand across concrete underfoot blended into the beach itself. Pella gaped up. The thing about the sky, the thing she always forgot, was the vaulting empty spaciousness of it. The blue or gray she'd seen framed through so many tinted windows, unbound now, explosive. Endlessly vaulting away from her eye.

And the sun, the enemy: horrible, impossible, unseeable.

"Look."

Raymond and David were pointing at the ruins behind them, the boardwalk, the blackened armatures of the abandoned amusement park. They didn't even look at the *sky*, Pella thought.

"See that tower, like a mushroom?" said Caitlin. "That was the parachute jump."

"Did you go on that one?" said Raymond.

"No. It was closed when I was young. Do you know why? People didn't open the parachutes in time, and broke their legs. But I rode the Cyclone."

"The what?"

"The roller coaster." Caitlin pointed it out, a cat's cradle of ravaged iron that looked helpless and naked in the sun.

Pella, annoyed, turned to the shore. To the right and left the beach was empty to the rock pilings that made, with the boardwalk, three walls of its frame. The fourth wall, the wrongest, was the sprawling, pitched ribbon of cyclone fence that ran between the pilings at the point of the water. Refuse and seaweed had washed up in the night and now clung, rotting, high on the wire, but at midday the waves fell far short of the base of the barrier.

Even this distance exhausted Pella's gaze, from the sand where she stood to the place past the fence where the darker sand met the sulfurous, glistening ocean. Even before she grappled with the edge where the water met the sky. Even before she grappled with the sky.

And now she was supposed to be able to look past that sky, into space. Caitlin wanted her to. But even the expanse of sand was space enough, too much.

Pella walked slowly away from her family and toward the water the fence would not allow her to reach. She kept her eyes lowered against the terrible sun, watched instead the strange track her cone made as it dragged in the sand.

"Pella!"

Her brothers came running up beside her, already out of breath, David almost tripping on his cone.

"Castle or fort?"

"What?" said Pella.

"Build a castle or a fort? David says castle, I say fort—"

"What's the difference?"

"C'mon, Pella—"

"No, I mean it, what's the difference between a castle and a fort?" Pella plumped down in the sand, her cone half-telescoping to accommodate her.

David fell on his knees alongside her. "I don't know."

Raymond began: "A fort is . . . ," but didn't continue.

Caitlin spread the blanket just behind them, and plopped down the bag of sandwiches and toys. "This a good spot? A fort is what, Ray?"

"They don't know the difference between a castle and a fort," said Pella, carefully leaving herself out of it.

Caitlin took a sandwich, then lifted her cone so that the bag was out, exposed on the blanket. "A castle is like a town. People live there, not just the king, or soldiers. It's permanent. A fort is a war thing, it's just for being attacked. But if you're building them in the sand maybe the difference is the castle is small and detailed, like a dollhouse, and a fort is like a big wall that *you* hide behind as if you were under attack."

"That's what I meant," said Raymond conclusively.

"Okay, fort," said David. He moved his cone to cover the bag of supplies and pulled out the spatula Caitlin had packed, for digging.

"Be careful of the sun," said Caitlin.

"We know," said Raymond, as they set to work.

Pella leaned back with her mother on the blanket, got as close as the cones would allow, and squinted through the far-off cyclone fence, at the waves.

Pella's first period was a glob of brownish red, as though some tiny animal had died against her body. It ruined a pair of underwear and sparked a fever of shame, and left behind a bland but dogged ache that woke her in the night. It was only then, as she lay awake in the dark, that she decided to tell Caitlin. Which led to a garish lesson in tampon insertion and a trip to the

UnderMall for a shopping splurge, as if Caitlin wanted to confirm Pella's private guess that this advance was a burden and required compensation.

"Raymond," said Caitlin, "get your hands inside the cone."

Clement's election was something worse, a collective shame, the family entombed like mummies in a sarcophagus of denial, imagining the polls weren't saying what they were, pretending not to overhear the phone calls, not to feel Clement's radiant dread. Then a truly pathetic night spent milling in a shabby ballroom, eyeing monitors, enduring sympathies first masked then slowly unmasked, like a party with the guest of honor gradually dying. Caitlin got drunk at the end, and Clement, unforgivably, didn't, instead stood clear-eyed and patronizing with a hand in Caitlin's hair as if to steady her, gazing self-pityingly off toward some imaginary frontier.

Not imaginary enough, it turned out.

Pella watched the boys play in the sand, saw them discover how hard it was to collaborate on a project from inside their separate cones. The cone rims kept slicing through towers and walls. As Pella watched, Raymond twisted his arm down into the sand up to the elbow.

"Tunnels!" he said.

David followed, and soon they'd built a tunnel that connected the space of their cones under the sand. "Look, Caitlin," said Raymond, as they triumphantly passed spatula, driftwood chunk, and plastic cup safely between them.

Pella thought of the tunnels through the bedrock of

the city. The decline of the subway was part of what cost Clement his seat, he'd explained. The people blamed his party for the collapses. The deaths. So they'd swept his party out of office.

And now were sweeping their family to the Planet of the Archbuilders. Or was it Caitlin who was doing that, with her talk?

"You can't do much at the *real* beach," complained Raymond when their tunnel pancaked, burying the tools in sand.

" 'Cause of these cones," said David.

"Soon you won't have to wear cones to go outside," said Caitlin. "That's one reason we're going."

"There's no sun?" said David.

"There's a sun, but it doesn't hurt you. The Archbuilders didn't ruin their ozone."

Pella looked involuntarily at Caitlin's bared arms through the translucent cone, at the three scars where cancers had been taken off.

"So why're we even here?" said Raymond. "If it's not as good as where we're going? Why didn't we just go to 'Scapes?"

"I wanted you to see the real beach, before we left. To look at the ocean. The Planet of the Archbuilders doesn't have an ocean."

"Huh," said Raymond.

Pella rose to this occasion. She saw, as Caitlin couldn't, that it was useless to try to inspire Raymond and David to certain feelings about the life of the family, about their own dawning lives. As useless as trying to inspire those feelings in dogs. Whether they would grow into such feelings or not, they were numb to them now.

And, though she was less clear on this, she thought Clement was half-numb to them too. They issued from Caitlin, and Pella was their only sure receptor. "Caitlin means that this is where she came when *she* was a kid," Pella said. "She used to swim here, come here all the time. So when you're doing that kind of stuff outdoors on the Planet of the Archbuilders you'll think of what it was like for her."

Though she spoke patiently, a part of Pella wanted to knock them down, to hold their eyes open and say, *Can't you see the sky? Can't you feel the change coming, the horizon growing closer?*

Clement was a coward not being here for this dry run under the sky. For Pella saw it now: This trip was on Clement's behalf. Caitlin was saying goodbye to her own Coney Island.

"Why do they have the fence in front of the water?" said Raymond.

"People were drowning themselves," said Caitlin.

"You mean that lemming thing," said Raymond.

"Yes," said Caitlin.

"That's stupid though," said Raymond. " 'Cause they always find a way. The fence won't stop them."

The lemming thing was another reason Clement and his party had lost the election. Pella had watched it on the news, bodies in water, massing and rolling like logs. Soldiers roaming afterward, aiming floodlights, pointlessly.

"That water's no good anyway," said Caitlin. "You can't swim in it. You barely could when I was a girl."

"But you did," said Raymond.

"Yup. And this beach was covered with people." Caitlin saw Pella glance at her scars again, and said, "Arms are so brave, don't you think?"

"What?" said Pella.

"Don't you think arms are brave?" She pistoned her right arm back and forth under the cone. "They just go on, they never get tired or give up or complain." She kneaded her bicep with her other hand. "It's the same arm I've had all my life, the same skin and muscles. It just goes pumping on into the future. Brave."

"I don't know," said Pella. But she looked at her own arm.

"You're crazy," said Raymond.

"Caitlin's not crazy," said David.

"I'm going to go look at the water anyway," said Raymond, getting up suddenly. "Maybe I can crawl under the fence."

"Stay where I can see you," said Caitlin.

"I'm going too," said David.

"You can see all the way to the rocks," said Raymond.

"Right. So don't climb on the rocks."

"Couldn't with this stupid cone anyway."

They pounded off through the sand, and Caitlin and Pella were left alone in their place, surrounded by a litter of digging tools and sandwich wrappings. The breeze dashed the tips of Pella's hair into her eyes.

Just a beat of silence passed between them, then Caitlin spoke.

"There's another thing about the Planet of the Archbuilders," she said. "It's something Ray and Dave might not understand."

Don't tell me, Pella thought instantly. She avoided her mother's eyes.

It was surely something peculiar and terrible when Caitlin had to begin by flattering her.

"We aren't going to be just any family moving there," Caitlin went on. "Clement is going to do Clement stuff wherever he goes. I mean, that's one part of why we're moving, so that he can."

"What's he going to do?"

"Nothing, at first. We're just going to move there. There's only a few settlers. We'll practically be the first. It's a chance to be there at the start of something, something very important."

Hearing her mother talk in circles, avoiding subjects, Pella suddenly wanted to be beside her, to move inside her cone. She wanted to protect and be protected at once.

"The thing is, for people to really live there, they have to live like the Archbuilders used to. There's this thing that happens to Archbuilders, young ones, and it would happen to people too. Except the people there now take a drug to keep it from happening."

"What thing?" said Pella.

"It's called becoming a witness," said Caitlin. "It happened to young Archbuilders, which there aren't so many of now. But it still happens."

It's going to happen to *me*, thought Pella. By telling only me she's going to make it happen to me.

"Nobody in our family is going to take the drug," said Caitlin. "Clement's looked into it, there's no danger. Just a chance to learn. It's something Clement and I feel strongly about."

Pella hated that policy talk, that Clement talk. *Feel strongly.* It was like Clement speaking out of Caitlin's mouth. Pella relied on her mother for words that were an antidote to Clement's.

"What does it do?"

"Well, what happens to *Archbuilders* is that the witness learns things about adults. I mean, the adult Archbuilders. It's a way of growing up. What happens to *people* we don't know, because nobody's tried it."

Caitlin said it like it was the most natural thing in the world. But why should Pella want to learn things about adults, let alone Archbuilders?

Why should she necessarily want to grow up?

After a pause, Pella said, "So how do they know anything happens? To people, I mean."

"Because it started to happen, a few times. But people panicked."

"What makes it happen?"

"It's something the Archbuilders created with their science. They made viruses, special ones. Only so long ago that it's like part of the planet now. Like a lot of things they did. Like the weather."

"So the people take drugs. Because they don't want to get an alien virus." This didn't sound exactly unreasonable to Pella. "That's what you mean by panicked."

17

Caitlin nodded, suddenly distracted. She squinted up the beach at Raymond and David, and said, "Something's wrong."

Raymond was at the corner, near the rocks, on the other side of the fence. David was halfway back, running toward them, and as Pella looked up he tripped over his cone and tumbled forward. He landed on his knees in the sand, his cone flattening up around him.

Caitlin rose and started out to meet him. Pella followed. They ran, cones wobbling around their ankles, to the place where David knelt.

He struggled up, his face flushed. "Raymond found something," he gasped.

"Let's go see," said Caitlin. She reached under his cone, exposing her own arms, and brushed the grit from his knees. "Come on."

"I'm scared," he said.

"That's okay," said Caitlin. "Let's go have a look." She nudged him along.

Pella got ahead. She could see something black, high on the rock barrier; Raymond was climbing toward it, on all fours, hampered by his cone.

Pella rushed closer, and the black thing grew clearer: It had an arm, which hung brokenly in the joint of two boulders. Three steps more, and it gained a head with blistered, purple cheeks. Pella stopped running, just short of the fence, then stepped forward, hypnotized, and put her hands on the mesh.

Caitlin and David came up behind her. Raymond was still climbing. Caitlin yelled his name, but the sound was almost swallowed in the surf's crash.

Again: "Raymond!"

He stopped there, a few feet below the body on the rocks, turned, and looked at them. Caitlin motioned with her hands. She couldn't wave, under the cone, but she pointed, first at him, then back, to the ground at her feet.

Raymond paused, then reversed, and picked his way back down the rocks, as slowly as he'd climbed. The waves smacked again and again just short of his path.

Pella gripped the fence and stared at the twisted black body on the rocks. So did Caitlin and David, now that Raymond was safely headed back. The man was purple and black and ruptured in places, and it was impossible to think of how he'd looked, alive. The sun and the ocean had each taken their blows.

As Raymond came off the rocks and started toward the fence David began weeping.

"I'm scared," said David again.

Raymond came up, the fence still between them. "What?" he said, to David. "Nothing happened."

"Come back under the fence," said Caitlin.

"The guy's dead," said Raymond. "He can't hurt anybody." But Pella saw that Raymond was trembling, actually.

"It's okay to be scared," said Caitlin. "It's scary, what you saw."

"He did the lemming thing, I guess," said Raymond. "The fence didn't stop him." He kicked more sand away from the place he'd scooted under, and squatted, crablike, holding the edges of his cone.

"It's not the lemming thing when it's only one person," said Pella. "It's just suicide."

"I want to go home," said David.

"We'll go home," said Caitlin. "But Raymond's right, nothing's going to hurt you." She turned David in his cone away from the fence. "It's just upsetting to see that, but nothing is going to happen. Be brave."

"Like an arm," said Raymond, laughing, nudging his brother's cone.

"Shut up," said David, sniffling.

"Anyway, Pella, he could have been part of some big lemming thing somewhere else and only his body washed up here," said Raymond. "The others floated—"

"Enough about that," said Caitlin.

"Shouldn't we report it?" said Raymond. They trudged together in a line, leaving the body on the rocks, and the adamant surf, behind them.

"We *will* report it," said Caitlin.

"Well that's all I was doing," said Raymond brightly. "I was checking for I.D."

"Okay, but I didn't want you to touch it, or get in the water. Come on."

Pella could hear that Caitlin was upset. They were all upset. But Pella felt only she knew it was a warning: dare to go out under the sky, dare to enter the sky, and trouble will touch you. Your tunnels will collapse. A body will fall.

Two

Pella showered first, rinsing away the grit that had found a place between her toes, letting the rain of drops on her eyelids batter away the vivid, scorched-in impressions of the dead black body and the high malicious sun, letting the whine of the hot-water pipe erase the echo of the ocean's crash, its awful hissing as it drew back over the sand. She soaked in her share of the hot water and more before blanketing herself in a towel. Then David took over the steamed-up bathroom, then Raymond. Caitlin waited until last.

Afterward, Pella would crazily think that if the order had been different, it would have happened to someone else, to the one who showered last. Someone besides Caitlin.

Pella and Raymond and David gathered, in their underwear, T-shirts, and wet hair, on the edge of their parents' bed, to watch television while Caitlin took her shower. A pile of fresh laundry lay in the center of the

21

bed, and Pella folded it while she watched. The show was David's choice, cartoons, which made it irksome that David wandered away in the middle. He went to the bathroom door and opened it, and the sound of Caitlin's shower obscured the voices coming from the television.

"*David,*" said Raymond.

"I heard something," said David. He went into the bathroom, left the door open.

Where was Caitlin's voice, shooing David out of the bathroom? Wondering absently, Pella turned to see, just as David emerged. Not rushing, not panicked like on the beach, but puttering, his hand near his mouth, almost as if he were looking for something on the floor.

"Pella?"

"What?"

"Caitlin made a funny face and fell down."

Pella went to the bathroom door. David tagged after her, but Raymond stayed at the television, ignoring them. Remembering later, it would seem to Pella a kind of protest, as though Raymond already knew and was registering his objection.

Pella went in. The shower poured down, but where was Caitlin? Pella moved the shower curtain.

Her mother lay splayed naked, filling the tub, slack, her eyes closed, mouth open, knees up, elbows jammed awkwardly at her sides, the surface of her stomach and breasts alive with the rain of water like a screen with static.

Pella stood shocked. The shower, curtain thrust aside, was wetting her T-shirt. She reached out dumbly and turned the shower control; the water poured out of the faucet instead, a gush over Caitlin's shoulder and neck. Caitlin's mouth was soft, as if she were speaking, forgetting a word. Her lips were beaded. The water rushed under her chin.

"Caitlin?" said Pella softly.

There was no reply, no response.

"Caitlin?" she said again. Then: "Mom?"

Nothing.

"Tell Raymond to call the hospital!" Pella shouted back at David, as she turned off the hot and cold. David ran away, mute. Pella had no idea if he'd heard.

The water drained away, droplets rolling off Caitlin's edges, leaving her wedged there. She lay still, but breathing, Pella saw. Her naked body seemed terribly big, a kind of world itself, a thing with horizons, places where Pella's gaze could founder, be lost.

Pella ordered her thoughts. Caitlin must have slipped, and hit her head.

The dead body at the beach—

No. No relation.

Where was Clement?

She put her hand in her mother's soaked hair, but couldn't find a gash or lump. Nothing, she thought, maybe this is nothing. She fell, she's okay, she's asleep, she'll wake up, she fell, she's okay, went Pella's little song of anguish. She touched her mother's chest, feeling the heartbeat, the dewy skin, the edge of her mother's breasts. Caitlin was so massively helpless, so impossible to protect.

She ran out to find David and bumped into Raymond, who'd been peering around the door's edge.

"I called 911," he said in a small voice. "They said we just have to get her into the subcar, and it'll go right to the hospital. They make it come, they have the address from the call."

"She's *naked,*" said Pella. "Anyway, we can't move her."

"We *have* to," said Raymond.

"Didn't you say we were kids?" said Pella. "Didn't you explain what happened?" Pella heard herself, thought: How could he explain what happened? Nothing happened. Nobody knows what happened.

David was sitting on the edge of their parents' bed, moaning, gasping for breath.

"Okay," said Pella, taking a breath. "David, stop crying. Call Clement's office."

"What if he isn't there?" David whined through his sobs.

"Then tell whoever *is* there. Raymond, come on."

Caitlin lay in exactly the same position. A rivulet of water ran down her nose. Pella took her nearest arm and pulled, drawing her shoulder up, peeling her with a pop of suction from the tub. Raymond went to the other end, and considered Caitlin's feet. Pella, with one knee on the edge of the tub, reached over and lifted Caitlin's other shoulder. Her mother's insensate head lolled forward.

Raymond was gingerly lifting Caitlin's calves, so her feet were aloft, nothing more. "She's just folding up," said Pella. "You have to lift her by the butt. This isn't funny."

"I'm not laughing," said Raymond.

He grimaced. They moved together, under Caitlin, and shifted her weight up and out of the tub, then immediately stalled and let her come to rest on the bath mat.

"We'll never get her down the stairs," said Pella.

"We have to."

They lifted her. Pella's breath rasped. She realized *she* was crying. Caitlin's arms flapped outward, and grazed the door frame as they passed through. But they didn't drop her. Willing it, they kept her off the floor, and moving along the hallway. In silence; Pella had no breath left for words of encouragement. Just David's crying in the next room, Raymond grunting as he worked to keep Caitlin's weight from slipping, her knuckles from clapping along the banister.

Caitlin's head rested crookedly against Pella's chest. Drops from her hair and crotch made a generous trail on the hallway floor, her body seemingly weeping. But Pella's tears evaporated as her cheeks heated with effort. Refusing to even stop and consider the challenge of the staircase, she groped backward with her foot and stepped down, nodding to Raymond to keep him coming.

One. Two. If she could manage to support Caitlin's weight for two steps, why not the rest? She leaned against the curved angle of the stairwell there at the top, her elbow sliding along the wall. Behind her she wouldn't be able to. But she shouldn't think of what was behind her. She watched her mother's stomach and breasts bunch obligingly as Raymond stepped down the first step himself, then felt the almost liquid weight of the body shifting, sliding out of her grasp again, folding toward the middle. She struggled to hold on, and to move backward, down another step. To unfold Caitlin. Caitlin's body.

"Pella!"

It was Clement, at the bottom of the stairs. Pella nearly fell backward. Raymond sank to his knees, and Caitlin's legs and buttocks settled on the second and third step.

"Something happened," Pella said, as Clement rushed up to meet them. The words were as specific as she felt possible.

"She hit her head," said Raymond. He hugged his mother's knees.

Clement lifted Caitlin away from them, staggering back for a moment against the banister with the weight and surprise. Pella felt a sting of satisfaction. You carry her. You be here in the first place.

"Did you call the hospital?" Clement said.

Pella nodded. "Raymond did." She stepped back up onto the landing beside her brother.

"We were putting her in the car," said Raymond, with a kind of anger.

Clement stood adjusting his position on the stairs, hoisting Caitlin higher in his arms, leaning back to balance the weight. He looked up from her face and nodded at Raymond. "I thought you were going to the beach," he said blankly. "I took a cab home."

"We got back hours ago," said Raymond.

Clement started downstairs, cradling Caitlin's head with his elbow, so it wouldn't dangle. Her eyes were still closed. Body limp. "Raymond, get a blanket and bring it down," Clement said. Raymond turned and darted back into the bedroom.

Pella followed dumbly, watching Clement struggle down the stairs, knowing she couldn't help. All the way down to the basement, where Clement loaded Caitlin into the car, her body filling the half-moon of the cabin's seats the way it had filled the bathtub: just fine if it weren't for arms and legs. Raymond arrived with a blanket.

"Should I come?" said Pella.

"You're in your underwear," Clement pointed out. "Stay here, watch David. I'll be back."

He closed the door, and instantly the system swept the car away, into the black tunnel. The train clattered like armor. Pella and Raymond stood idiotically mute, their task abolished. Pella didn't know how to honor this moment, the sudden emptiness where her parents had been, the emergency suspended. She couldn't cry. She and Raymond had made themselves taut for the task on the stairs; it didn't matter that Clement had intercepted Caitlin. They wouldn't cry. Raymond actually seemed furious. Without speaking, they went back upstairs to see David. He was probably crying, and that would do.

But no, he wasn't crying. He sat watching television, rapt, as though the television could sew up the rift of what had happened. It was so fast, Pella thought. Caitlin had been felled and had vanished from the house in the space between two sets of commercials.

Pella didn't speak to David, didn't risk disturbing

him. She sat down on the edge of the bed beside him and lifted her knees up to make a shelf for her chin and watched. In a moment Raymond joined them, and they sat there together staring, right through the commercials, to the end of the show. When it was over Pella changed the channel. Raymond and David didn't argue about the program, just sat watching stonily.

Clement came home alone. When he walked into the bedroom Pella switched off the television.

"She's still at the hospital," he said, answering the obvious question, but in a mumbling, turned-inward way, as though he doubted it himself.

"Did she wake up?" said Pella.

"A little," Clement said. "She seemed confused. They want to examine her."

"You talked to her?"

"I talked to her, yes. She couldn't really talk to me." He weighed this mild irony for a moment, blinking.

"She must of really gotten knocked out," said Raymond hopefully.

"They don't know what happened," said Clement. "Her head isn't hurt. The bruises are on her back." He looked down at the floor, then away, but not at them. The bedful of his worried children. Pella saw her father extending the self-pitying gloom that had enclosed him since the election defeat to cover this new crisis: Caitlin's fall was something happening to *him*. No matter that he hadn't been there, and they had.

"That's stupid," said Raymond. "You can't get knocked out from hitting your back."

"Well maybe she wasn't knocked out," said Pella. "Maybe something else happened."

"She slipped in the tub," said Raymond angrily.

"David saw it," said Pella. "Not you."

That got Clement's attention. "David?" he said.

"He heard a noise," said Pella. "Before she fell down. That's why he went in."

They all looked at David, who stared back, spooked.

"He *thought* he heard something," said Raymond.

"Caitlin made a funny face," said David. "Before she fell down."

"What do you mean, *funny?*" said Raymond.

"Quiet, Ray," said Clement. "Tell me what you saw, David. You saw her fall?"

David nodded.

Clement was stirred. He stared at his children, seeming to grasp for the first time their presence in this episode in his life. He moved nearer and gathered their heads and shoulders under his hands. Pella felt his hand on her skull and a thrill of animal comfort went through her.

"Why did you go in?" Clement said softly to David. "You heard something?"

"Caitlin said something," said David carefully. "Then I saw her making a face."

"It doesn't mean anything," said Raymond harshly, even as he leaned against his father's stomach.

"Maybe," said Clement. "Maybe it does."

"David probably imagined it," said Raymond.

Clement stepped away, his hands slipping across the children's shoulders, dropping to his sides. He moved awkwardly, like a stranger in his own bedroom. Pella took hold of David's hand.

Clement stood not speaking before them for a moment, then picked up the phone and left the room. He stopped outside the door. Pella heard him dial, ask to talk to Dr. Flinch or Finch.

David sat still on the bed, his hand limp in Pella's grasp. Raymond sat forward and switched the television back on.

"She just fell and hit her *head,*" he said, not looking at them. It was like he was angry at the television show.

Three

Clement left the three of them in Caitlin's hospital room, and went to find her doctor. Caitlin's head was wrapped, but only because they'd shaved her for tests. They hadn't operated, yet.

The room was sterile and almost completely without character, but what Pella hated most savagely about it were the few details that made it particular. The moon-shaped crack in the ceiling tile, the stain on the wall that looked like urine, the torn calendar. All the things that made it Caitlin's room instead of someone else's, some other sick person unknown.

Caitlin sat up, a book across her legs, her bed cranked up so it was nearly a high-backed chair.

"Listen to this," she said. " 'The remaining Arch-builders possess an extraordinary linguistic capacity; it is the last manifestation of their former complexity, the richness that has otherwise faded from their culture.' " Her hair gone, Caitlin's face showed its lines. But it glowed, too, despite the flat white hospital light. Her lips were chapped, and she licked them as she spoke. " 'They have nearly fifteen thousand independent languages native to their planet, and the average Archbuilder speaks five to eight *percent* of these'—that's *hundreds* of languages—"

David clambered up on her bed and put his head on her legs just under the book.

Caitlin put her hand in David's hair and went on. " 'The fruit of their fascination with English is that it is now one of the seven or eight languages any two Archbuilders, meeting as strangers, are likeliest to have in common.' "

"David isn't interested in this," said Raymond hopefully.

"Why do they like English?" said Pella.

"Here, wait, it says something good about that." Caitlin flipped pages back. "Here. 'Archbuilders describe English as a language of enchanting limitations. The English vocabulary is tens of thousands of words smaller than any language native to their planet. English words seem, to an Archbuilder, garishly overloaded with meaning. One Archbuilder describes speaking English as "stringing poems into sentences," another compares it to "speaking hieroglyphs." ' "

Caitlin was unstoppable now. Pella's family was distorting, wrenching itself into a new shape in two realms: Caitlin's strange, rebelling body, her illness; and the impending move, the frontier that seemed to be rushing to swallow them like a horizon in motion. The point of relation between these realms, the arrow of causality, was obscured. Was Caitlin hurrying to prepare them for a life without her? She'd begun her cheerleading for the Planet of the Archbuilders before she fell and turned sick, so it couldn't be that. If anything, the reverse. Moving to the Planet of the Archbuilders was the family project, and the family included Caitlin, didn't it? So she was going, which meant she would recover and be fine.

When Pella sensed herself relying on such logic, she was almost nauseous.

One thing was certain. Caitlin's illness was the unspoken text of their days, and the move to the Planet of the Archbuilders was the spoken. It filled so much time that Pella wondered if they even had to make the trip. They were living it here, in Caitlin's hospital room, each time they visited.

"Let me tell you about the household deer," Caitlin said. She flopped the book over, began paging through it in chunks. The huge pages made her hands look tiny and feeble. "I was just reading about that."

"Household deer?" sighed Raymond, as though he knew he might as well express interest since he would be forced to listen either way.

"Yes, they're like mice, really. We'll have them, in our new house. They're everywhere, they live everywhere the Archbuilders do. Listen—"

"Pella?" It was Clement, looking in. Dr. Flinch stood in the hall behind him, respectfully back, granting the family space.

"What?"

"Come here. Leave the boys with Caitlin." He

grinned and waved, as though he were somehow barred from entering the room. "We'll be back."

Pella got up from her chair. In the hall, Clement held out his arm to her. She glanced back; Caitlin roughed David's hair and started, "The household deer—"

Pella followed Clement and Dr. Flinch down the hall, and Caitlin's voice was lost in echoey hospital murmurs and clatter. Pella was sorry to leave Raymond and David alone with Caitlin. Their mother's judgment had somehow gotten worse, and she was boring and mystifying and frightening them with her talk. Two weeks before she had been enchanting Raymond and David with Archbuilders, making them laugh and filling them with real anticipation even when they didn't really understand. Now she was didactic, awful.

Clement stopped Pella, a hand on her shoulder. They'd come to an empty place in the hall, near a vacant nursing station. "I want you to hear this," said Clement, looking from Pella to the doctor.

Then I don't want to hear it, Pella thought instantly. It was a poor way for Clement to start.

"Pella?" said Dr. Flinch. His nose was enormous, his chin creased. It made his entire face a huge exclamation mark. "Am I saying your name right? Your father tells me you're a very mature thirteen years old. And very smart."

Very, very, quite contrary, thought Pella. But she said, "I guess."

"I was telling your father about what we learned from your mother's tests in the last few days. There are two different kinds of brain tumors, Pella—I mean, of course, there are thousands, no two are alike—but for our immediate purposes there are just two."

"Uh-huh."

"One is like a marble sitting in a bowl of Jell-o. It doesn't belong there, but it keeps to itself. Doesn't mix with the Jell-o. That kind is easy, because you can pretty much just"—he made a pinching motion with his forefinger and thumb—"pluck it out."

You shouldn't talk to someone like they were a baby when the subject was brain tumors, Pella thought. If you thought they were still a baby you shouldn't discuss brain tumors, and if you didn't think they were still a baby, you shouldn't talk that way. But Pella didn't know how to tell Dr. Flinch to stop.

Or on which grounds.

"—other kind is like a stain of ink in the Jell-o. The ink mixes with the Jell-o everywhere it touches. There aren't any edges. You can't"—Dr. Flinch's new hand motion depicted frustrated, uncertain scissors—"know where to cut."

"Caitlin has the second kind," said Clement. Then he rubbed his nose as if he was embarrassed, had spoken out of turn.

"What happens to people with that?" said Pella.

There was a giggling in the hall. Pella turned around. Raymond and David were on their hands and knees, scuffling along the tile of the corridor. A nurse with a cart of meal trays skirted past them, humming to herself obliviously.

"Boys," said Clement.

"Don't talk to us," said Raymond, looking up quickly. "We're household deer." He tittered. Grinning at the floor, the two boys crawled in a tight circle around Clement's legs, then Pella's.

"Go back to Caitlin's room," said Pella.

"We're pretending because she *told* us to," said David, voice rising in a lunatic laugh at the end, his head still ducked almost against Raymond's buttocks as he crawled.

"Yeah, anyway, household deer are almost invisible," said Raymond.

Pella saw the distance, the unreachableness in Raymond's eyes.

"Well, you're *hospital* deer, and you're completely visible," said Clement. "Go back to Caitlin. Come on." He scooted them back toward her room. He seemed grateful for the interruption, though, his own unbearable giddiness justified by the moment of child's play. "We'll be back in a minute."

The boys crawled away and through Caitlin's doorway. Pella imagined Clement crawling off after them.

"What great kids," said Dr. Flinch, shaking his head, his expression tortured. Men want problems to be theirs alone, Pella thought. The doctor seemed to want pity, as though this young mother's illness was difficult for doctors in a way the family couldn't understand.

The same way Clement wanted the election to be his private loss, when it belonged to all of them.

"Yes," said Clement.

"What happens to people with that?" said Pella again, demanding the doctor acknowledge her. Clement was currently useless to Pella. Probably to anyone. Pella knew this version of Clement, the hopeless one who bumbled in a group of three or four people at one side of an auditorium, before stepping up to the podium to deliver a speech that four thousand found riveting and brilliant.

Except there was no podium, no four thousand now. Just the bumbling.

"What?" Flinch straightened his face, tried to smile at Pella.

"Stain in Jell-o," she insisted. She stared at Dr. Flinch's hands. His forefinger was covered with tiny pen-marks, little hatches. He will reach into Caitlin's head, Pella thought.

"She is a little grown-up, isn't she?" said Flinch, grimacing at Clement, looking for help.

Clement didn't reply.

"Yes, well, I want to be perfectly truthful," said the doctor. "Everything depends on the specifics, and the specifics are what we don't know. Many people with your mother's illness fight it again and again throughout their lives. No drug or radiation can ever completely eliminate the cancer. But people live years . . ."

Or they don't, Pella understood.

It would forever be linked for Pella to the collapse of the subway. The tunneling devices that had hollowed out too much of the city's bedrock, the failed surgical incursion that had destroyed Caitlin, taken too much of her with the tumor, left her half-paralyzed and inarticulate and dying anyway. Hollowed. Why couldn't she go on reading to them about the Planet of the Archbuilders forever? That would have been a reasonable compromise. They could have moved into the hospital, moved into the dayroom with the crossword puzzles, barricaded Caitlin's room against the doctors. Instead, when she was returned to the ward everything had mysteriously changed in the unseen operating room, a corner had been turned without any explanation, and now they were supposed to say goodbye and it was to a Caitlin who wasn't herself, wasn't even whole. Her smile drooped. Her words were thick, frustrated. Clement took them out of school, and every day for ten days they came in the morning for Caitlin's dwindling minutes of clarity, to hold her hand and hear her try to say she loved them. The Planet of the Archbuilders was never mentioned, though Pella saw that Clement was still quietly making the preparations. The four of them were hypnotized by Caitlin's fall in slow-motion. Every day she had a little less time. Every day there was less said, less to say. Every day for ten days they watched her fall asleep and afterward went to the hospital cafeteria, where Clement bought sandwiches and ice cream that the four of them, the incomplete family, ate in stunned and grateful silence.

Time heals, give it some time, what these poor kids need is time: At the funeral everyone spoke of sorrow and time, and then Clement led his motherless children and their sorrow aboard a tiny ship where they were frozen alive for a trip that lasted twenty months, but seemed to them an eye blink, a dream. So had they been given time? Or was their sorrow frozen with them? Raymond and David and Pella, short a mother, and Clement, short a constituency, and a wife. It was as though Clement had replaced Caitlin with the ship. As though they had tunneled inside her departing body for comfort and escape. Then hurtled with it into the void.

Joe Kincaid
Ellen Kincaid
Bruce Kincaid (13)
Martha Kincaid (8)

Snider Grant
Laney Grant
Doug Grant (15)
Morris Grant (8)

Llana Richmond
Julie Concorse
Melissa Richmond-
Concorse (15)

Hiding Kneel
Truth Renowned
Lonely Dumptruck
Gelatinous Stand

Efram Nugent
Ben Barth
Diana Eastling
E.G. Wa
Hugh Merrow

II

THE PLANET *of the*

ARCHBUILDERS

Four

"Who's that kid?" said Raymond, pointing out the figure trailing behind, the clumsy shadow they'd all noticed.

A group had formed this morning, children wandering out into the valley together, away from the homes, beneath the empty sky. Pella, Raymond, and David Marsh, Bruce and Martha Kincaid.

Bruce Kincaid was the same age as Pella. Martha was eight, a year older than David. The Kincaids had lived here months already. They picked their way blithely over the crumbled ground, distorted shadows dancing, through the tendrils of dried dead vines. The new children, the Marshes, walked cowed, stealing apprehensive glances at the blazing sky.

"That's just Morris," said Martha Kincaid lightly, not even turning to look at the boy who was tracking them.

"Morris Grant," said Bruce. "He's a real pain. He's

the only other kid besides us. That's why it's good you're here."

"He has an older brother," said Martha.

"Yeah, but Doug doesn't hang around with us," said Bruce to Pella and Raymond, ignoring his sister. "He's fifteen."

The *real pain* tailed them out into the valley, staying on the path but keeping a safe distance behind. Whenever Pella looked at him, Morris Grant would turn and start throwing rocks off to one side, as if that were all he was there for, as if he weren't following.

Morris Grant's missiles kicked up little plumes of dust where they landed, ineffectually near no matter how hard he threw. Pella was transfixed, her neck already sore from turning her head, her eyes bedazzled by distance, by trying to measure the valley. Was it all stones and ruin? Where did the Archbuilders sleep? Where were the Archbuilders?

Pella hadn't seen one yet.

"Look," said Bruce Kincaid. He kicked at a green vine that sprang from the scabbed, rocky ground. "You want to see where the potatoes come from?"

"Potatoes?" said Pella.

David knelt and tugged on the vine.

"Careful," said Bruce. He nudged David away with his foot. "Yeah, you know, Archbuilder food. *Everybody's* food. You guys ate it at our house last night."

"That wasn't potatoes," said Raymond.

"Yes it was. Archbuilder potatoes. That stewy stuff was sour potatoes mixed with meat potatoes, and the vegetable, like broccoli tops? Green potatoes."

"Show them about fish potatoes," said Martha Kincaid, gasping with pleasure at this prospect.

"Gotta find one first," said Bruce. He knelt and began smoothing pebbles and dirt away from the crevice, holding the vine gently to one side. David put his hands out to help, but Bruce said, "Look out," and unfolded a large pocketknife.

"Dad said you're gonna ruin your pocketknife keep chopping at rocks," said Martha.

"I like to sharpen it," said Bruce absently, prizing the knife into the gap. His tongue arched out onto his left cheek as he worked.

The night before, the night of their arrival, Clement and Pella and Raymond and David had been invited to eat at the Kincaids' house. The new world outside was boundless and dark, impossible to see or think about. The Marshes rushed from their strange empty new house to the Kincaid's like escaping slaves, huddled against the universe, hurrying from one puny light to another, eyes lowered, mouths shocked dumb. Pella held David's hand. Raymond walked a little ahead across the shadowed crust of ground, daring himself, pushing away from the family.

Be brave like an arm, Pella thought.

Bruce and Martha's parents, Joe and Ellen Kincaid, cooked a big meal of Archbuilder food. They hadn't called it potatoes. The two families sat and ate together in the small house, and Pella felt an irrational fury at the adult Kincaids, for presuming they *were* meeting the

Marsh family when Caitlin wasn't there. Pella knew Caitlin would have talked more than anyone, would have dominated this table and the talk at it, as she always had. Listening to Clement's clumsy overtures was painful. Couldn't the Kincaids hear how incapable he was? Apparently not. This was what passed for adult conversation on the Planet of the Archbuilders.

At that dinner Bruce Kincaid had right away latched onto Pella, appointed himself her guide, distracting her from Clement. Sitting beside her at the table, he pointed out the household deer that hid in the shadows at the edges of the room, watching the families eat. "There—there. Do you see them?"

It took her a while to make out the tiny figures, more miniature quicksilver giraffe than *deer*. But climbing giraffe, able to cling, like the one on the side of Joe Kincaid's desk or the one that scurried up the edge of the curtain. Bruce showed her how they hid in darkness and reflections. He switched the lights in the room on and off so the household deer were surprised, and briefly more visible, before they adjusted to the new lighting. After a few minutes Ellen Kincaid said, "Bruce, stop that flashing, please. It's giving me a headache," and when he stopped the creatures were again almost invisible. But Pella's eyes had begun learning to find them.

Before dessert, Ellen Kincaid brought out a large plastic bottle and put a capsule of blue powder at each child's place at the table. Clement quickly palmed up those lying before Pella and David and Raymond and handed them back to her, comically swift and elegant, before she'd even screwed the top back on the bottle.

It was the drug to stop the Archbuilder viruses from living in their bloodstreams.

"I know, it's better to do it with the food," Ellen Kincaid said, misunderstanding. "But keep these. You can give us some of yours later. We all share around here, anyway—"

Clement held up his hand. "We're not . . ."

Ellen Kincaid waited, but Clement didn't finish.

"Excuse me," said Ellen Kincaid.

Pella felt a disconcerting pride in Clement, his plans, his notions, his courteous stubbornness. It was the pride Caitlin would have felt if she were here, so Pella felt it on Caitlin's behalf. Clement's notions made their family somehow matter. Even damaged. Even here.

There was a clumsy silence, then Joe Kincaid brought out the dessert, a mashed thing, like a hat with powdered sugar. He set it down, and Ellen Kincaid passed him one of the rejected capsules. The Kincaids all swallowed theirs, Martha Kincaid with her wondering eyes locked on Pella.

Clement then changed the unspoken subject, began to speak of gardening, his admiration for the Kincaids' garden, his hope that he could start one himself. Bruce caught Pella's attention at the same time, and the table split again into two conversations, adults and children. The pills were forgotten. Or at least not spoken of again.

After dinner the exhausted family trudged across flat stones behind Joe Kincaid and his flashlight, back to their own house, to fall into hard new beds and instantly asleep. Pella dreamed of the subway, as if to bring the darkness of the empty sky close around her, to make a tunnel of it. A hiding place.

The next morning Bruce Kincaid arrived early, to carry on his job of stewardship by leading Pella and her brothers out into the valley.

The settlement was at the farthest edge of a basin ringed by crumbled arches. Eroded spires that rose a thousand feet into the air. Fallen bridges, incomplete towers, demolished pillars. The valley was a monumental roofless cathedral with only the buttresses intact, and the calm purple-pink sky of the Planet of the Archbuilders glowed like stained-glass windows between these vast ruined frames.

Caitlin had explained it all, narrating from her hospital bed. Her voice hung over this landscape. So Pella knew that the towers were unnecessary, ornamental, that they had only ever been partly habitable. And that no one, human or Archbuilder, lived in them now. What rooms existed were mostly filled with rubbish, the dead-end flotsam of the Archbuilders' abandoned civilization. The towers and arches were built into the rocky floor of the valley, where landscaping viruses had sewn ground and architecture together.

Here in sight of the ruins, Pella understood why the creatures still called themselves Archbuilders. Even if that part of them had gone to sleep—if anything, it would make it more urgent that they advertise their connection to the spires, to the network of ruins. In remembrance. They were like ghosts haunting the abandoned mansion of their own civilization.

So what were the human families? Ghosts haunting someone else's mansion?

The children wandered out among the pitted hills in the middle of the valley, as far from the shadows of the arches as possible. Pella had to work not to feel doomed out under the open sky, had to struggle not to cringe under the sun. Caitlin is here, she told herself. Their mother had died and brought them here, insisted on their coming, weaving her tale of this place into her dying. So she must be here. They must have come to find her in this landscape, somewhere in these rocks and ruins, somewhere between the flat valley and the bowed sky. Like the Archbuilders, Caitlin had left but was still here, in this landscape of remembrance. Pella squinted, lifted her head defiantly, ignored the sun.

It was their first day.

Bruce scooped out around a wide flat stone with his knife until it was loose enough to pry up. To Pella's surprise, there was a sucking sound, like a shoe pulled out of mud. Bruce grunted, and flipped the rock over. The little vine led down into a moist crevice, where it turned into a yellow-green lace of veins covering a rubbery, translucent sac. Bruce took his knife and carefully slit the outer hide of the sac, then reached in and began separating the pods that nestled inside.

They crowded around, even Morris Grant, who'd

crept up on the edge of the group once they'd stopped. Nobody seemed to object that he'd joined them. They just ignored him. He looked harmless enough to Pella.

"Here. C'mon, Martha," said Bruce Kincaid. He lifted out the first subsection and handed it to his sister. "That's a green potato." Martha held it out with two hands and everyone took a turn poking at it. "Split it open and cook it and you get that stuff we ate with the sauce on it. See, but this one's a cake potato." He gave the next one to Raymond. "They all grow together. It's called a cake potato, but it isn't sweet. The Arch-builders mostly eat those ones. I don't like them unless they're all covered with butter and sugar, like the one we had for dessert. Even then I don't like them much."

"Me neither," said Martha.

Pella felt the cake potato. It was heavy, and it dented, like an avocado. Nothing like *potato*, or *cake*, as she knew them. For what that was worth.

Morris Grant said, "That's no big deal. That stuff is everywhere."

Bruce Kincaid barely glanced at the smaller boy. "Yeah, but they haven't seen it, so shut up, Morris."

"Can I have one?" said David.

Bruce, still squatting, pulled another pod from the crevice in the rocks. "Sour potato."

"How many different kinds?" said David.

Bruce said: "Sour, meat, green, cake—"

"And fish!" said Martha.

"I'm getting to that," said Bruce. "Sour, meat,

green, cake, tea, uh, ice, and fish. Fish and ice are the hardest to find. Fish is the weirdest one."

"How do they grow in there?" said David.

"Long time ago the Archbuilders took all their favorite foods and made them grow like this, under the ground, so they wouldn't ever have to do any work. Efram says that's what made them all lazy and stupid."

"Who's Efram?" said Pella.

"Efram won't eat the potatoes," continued Bruce, not quite answering the question. "Everybody else eats them, even if they're trying to grow something else. But not Efram. He's got Ben Barth working on his farm like a slave to get out enough food that isn't Archbuilder potatoes."

Pella heard adult words echoed unreflectingly in Bruce Kincaid's speech.

"Efram who?" she said.

Raymond and David were prying at the cake potato, trying to break the skin, reducing the thing to a bag of pulp in the process.

"Efram Nugent," said Bruce. "He's not around now, or you'd of met him. He's always out roaming around. That's why Ben Barth's got to run his farm."

"Efram discovered the Planet of the Archbuilders," said Morris Grant, a little defiantly.

"Did not, Morris," said Bruce. "Don't be stupid."

Morris Grant turned and sidearmed a rock into the cracked valley.

"Show them fish potatoes, Bruce," said Martha.

"Okay, okay. I've got to find one first." Bruce went

back to gouging in the crevice. He rejected a series of potatoes, piling them gently to one side, then said, "Here." He held it out. Raymond reached out with extended hands, but Bruce said, "No, cradle it. Like a water balloon." He plumped it against Raymond's chest.

"Take the others," he said, and distributed the pile among Pella, David, Martha, and Morris. "E. G. Wa gives us a nickel for every potato we bring in. He bottles them and makes soup and stuff. Except tea potatoes—he's always got too many of those. A nickel *credit*, that is. Forget that one." He indicated the cake potato that Raymond and David had been struggling with. "You ruined it. It's crap."

"I'm keeping the credit for the ones I carry," said Morris.

"Jeezus," said Bruce. "Whatever."

"Credit where?" said Raymond.

"E. G. Wa has kind of a shop," said Bruce. "Much as you can have a shop with thirteen people in the entire valley. Seventeen now that you're here."

"I thought there wasn't any money here," said Raymond.

"Well, E. G. Wa and some other folks still use dollars and cents, just out of habit, I guess," said Bruce Kincaid. "But mostly everybody just trades."

"Also the Archbuilders sometimes buy stuff," said Martha. "Wa gives them money for bringing potatoes."

"Yeah, it's kind of stupid," said Bruce. "He gives them money, then takes it back. But it gives them something to do."

Archbuilders sounded less than impressive. Pella

decided she would be as casual about them as Bruce and Martha Kincaid.

The six children trudged back across the valley, arms loaded with various potatoes, Raymond cradling just the one sloshy fish potato. Morris trailed, taking care to indicate his apartness from the group even as he joined them in the errand. They turned away from the path back to both the Kincaids' house and to Pella and Raymond and David's new home, and headed down a series of crumbled steps until those houses were out of sight.

E. G. Wa's shop was just the front part of his house, which was itself just another of the prefabricated cabins they all seemed to have for homes. Where the Kincaids had their dinner table, Wa had a counter loaded with jars. Against the wall was a small table with an optimistically full pot of coffee heating on a burner, and arrayed for the nonexistent coffee drinkers were three rocking chairs.

As the six of them came clumping in from the porch, Pella caught sight of a pair of household deer skittering out of sight behind the counter.

"Look," said Bruce, pointing to a shelf loaded with packages, foil- and plastic-wrapped goods imprinted with advertising logos. "My mother bakes this bread, see?" Now Pella saw the dusty loaves, more plainly wrapped in transparent plastic. "She trades it to Wa, and he sells it out of the shop."

"But we get it free at home," added Martha.

Pella had a sudden pang of hunger. For bread, for mother.

E. G. Wa came out of the back. He was tall, and his smile had a permanent, mummified look. He angled his spindly body over the counter and surveyed the group of children. After a moment he took the toothpick out of his mouth and said, "These the new kids, Brucey?"

"Uh-huh."

"Got stuff for me already?"

"Yeah." Bruce lumped his armload of potatoes onto the counter, then helped the others do the same, except for Raymond, and Morris, who managed alone.

E. G. Wa pointed his toothpick at the potato Raymond held. "That a fish?"

"Yeah, we're keeping it," said Bruce.

"Give a quarter for that one."

"Nope."

"Ha-ha. You bargaining, young Mr. Kincaid?"

"No, we want it."

Martha whispered, too loud, to Pella, "He makes soup of it. It's yucky."

"Okay," said E. G. Wa, "fifteen, thirty, forty-five—you got seventy cents here."

"Morris's are separate," said Bruce, with sardonic emphasis.

"Fifty-five and fifteen, then," said E. G. Wa. "Dollar seventy-five for you with what you had before, Brucey."

"Give me a package of those cookies," said Bruce, pointing.

"Yes, sir! Earth imports. Good deal trading Archbuilder crap for nice Earth stuff, eh? Only problem is the Archbuilder emigration tax—that's fifteen cents per new kid in town, comes to, uh—"

"Cut it out," said Bruce. He rapped his knuckles against the counter directly over the cookies. "He's just making that stuff up," he said to Pella and Raymond. "There's no such thing as Archbuilder tax."

"Hah." E. G. Wa gestured honorifically with toothpick in hand, then pulled out the package of cookies. "Very good, Mr. Kincaid. And what's the names of you new kids?"

"Pella Marsh," said Pella, just as Raymond said, "Raymond." E. G. Wa nodded, though it seemed unlikely he had made them out. And then Pella added, "And David."

They went out and sat on the porch, Raymond with the fish potato resting in his lap. Bruce crinkled open the cookies and handed them out, two to each, except to Morris.

"Hey," said Morris.

"It was your idea to keep yours separate," said Bruce.

"Fifteen cents isn't enough to buy anything."

"It was your idea."

"You can build up credit," said Martha consolingly. "Like Bruce did."

"Yeah, but make sure Wa writes your fifteen cents down," said Bruce. "He'll forget it."

"He didn't forget yours."

"Well I'm in there all the time." Bruce said this through a mouthful of cookies. Morris glared resentfully.

Pella gave Morris one of her cookies. He didn't thank her, just wolfed it down, then scooped up some rocks to throw from the porch into the gully. After a minute he said, "Potatoes growing out everywhere, I don't even get why he gives you any credit at all."

"It's work digging them up, something you wouldn't know about," said Bruce. "Worth a nickel to him. That's the reason."

Pella thought she knew a better reason, having to do with the full pot of coffee and the empty rocking chairs.

"Fish, fish, fish," said Martha softly.

"Okay," said Bruce, exasperated. "Let's go. We'll do it at your house," he said to Pella and Raymond. "You can keep them."

"Keep them?"

"You'll see."

Clement wasn't there when they went in. Bruce rummaged confidently through the cabinets in the kitchen of the new homestead until he found a large glass jar. Pella and Raymond and David sat and waited, still as much strangers in this house as the other children. The fish potato sat waiting on the kitchen table, quivering slightly when someone walked nearby.

Bruce filled the half-gallon jar two-thirds full with water from the well tap at the sink, put it on the table, and sawed a small hole in the top of the potato with his pocketknife. Pinching the rupture shut, he tilted the potato up, then opened his fingers and squeezed the contents into the water like a baker writing with a bag of frosting.

Seven little bodies flooded out into the jar. Sardines with legs. They drifted toward the bottom, but before the first bumped down it was beginning to squirm and thrash. Within a minute they had untangled and begun swimming around inside the jar in frantic darting movements, and the amniotic gunk that floated away from their bodies dissolved and made the water gray. Bruce took it to the sink, and covering the top with his fingers poured off most of the floating sediment, then refilled the jar from the tap with fresh water.

"There."

Even Martha, who had obviously seen this before and had been clamoring to have it demonstrated to others, crowded closer. And Morris forsook his distance to have a look. Everyone peered in at the swimmers. The legs of the fish groped back and down, like swimmers searching for the bottom in the deep end of a pool, and though their tiny blistered eyes were still shut they avoided collisions with one another or the walls of the jar.

"You can feed them whatever," said Bruce. "They don't grow or anything, you can't train them. They'll die, eventually."

"That guy makes soup out of them?" said Raymond, incredulous. "That makes me want to retch."

"It's pretty rotten soup," agreed Bruce. "But they make pretty bad pets. Efram says they're not real animals, just some kind of screwed-up Archbuilder food thing. All the potatoes are just stuff the Archbuilders wanted to have big supplies of around to eat."

"Why are they alive, then?" said Raymond, his forehead screwed up. It was an urgent question.

"Maybe the way you can wake them up if you put them in water is just some weird mistake."

"The Archbuilders eat them," suggested Pella. She understood Raymond's objection. She too wanted the confusing and horrible fish to have a clear place in the order of things.

"Nope," said Bruce. "The Archbuilders ignore them. When they dig them up they throw them out in the sun to rot. That's why Efram says that it's a mistake."

"Only E. G. Wa eats it," said Martha, wrinkling her mouth and nose. "In soup."

"Dad eats the soup sometimes," said Bruce. "Ben Barth eats it too, when Efram's not around. E. G. Wa's always handing it out when you go in there—probably *all* the grown-ups eat it sometimes."

The assertion went unanswered.

"Speaking of *not eating,*" said Morris Grant to Pella, "Martha told me you're not eating the pills." The words could have been neutral, but his voice rose tauntingly at the end.

"Mind your own business," said Bruce.

"Martha told me."

"Then Martha should mind *her* own business."

"Efram isn't going to like it," said Morris.

"Efram isn't their dad."

Pella felt she should speak up, not leave it to Bruce, but she didn't know what she would be defending, what it meant to the people here that her family wasn't taking the little blue pills. It was her battle, inherited from Caitlin, but she didn't understand it.

David sat with his chin resting on his crossed arms, staring at the swimming figures inches away.

Morris went to the door. "I'm telling Efram."

"Efram isn't even *around*," said Bruce. "You can go tell anybody you want. Tell some old Archbuilder. Get out of here." He moved suddenly at Morris, stomping on the floor threateningly. Morris shrank through the doorway out onto the porch. "Go, already," said Bruce.

Morris peered through the door once more, then ran away over the porch and off into the paths of the valley.

Raymond went out of the kitchen, into his new room. David just sat hypnotized by the things in the jar.

"But what's going to happen?" said Martha to Pella.

"What?"

"If you don't take the pills."

"I don't know," said Pella.

Five

"Misplaced intensity," said Hiding Kneel.

Hiding Kneel was the first Archbuilder the girl had seen in the flesh—flesh and fur and shell and frond. In fact flesh was barely visible, just the black leather of its ears and eyelids. Whereas the fur was everywhere, under the papery clothes, and it was black, too, smooth and tufted, perhaps faintly musky. Shell shone beneath the fur in odd places, sleek natural armor; cheeks, wrists, what might be breastplates. The Archbuilder's fronds seemed less horns or hair or limbs than flowers, a bundle of calla lilies topping the Archbuilder's head, twisted, drooping elegantly to the side, tucked behind the large, clownish ears. The fronds were a kind of rhyming rebuke to the smashed towers that littered the planet: Bend, they said, and you may not crumble.

The girl and her brother had been sitting on the porch, gazing at the distant arches, when a pickup truck rumbled over the wastes, driven by the man named Ben

Barth. Their father sat in the cab. Hiding Kneel rode in the back of the truck, with the supplies. When the truck stopped beside the porch, the Archbuilder clambered out in a supple, slinking motion, its limbs seeming to flow in a ripple of two-way knee joints, of double elbows.

The girl felt the sight of the Archbuilder move through her, a physical thing. She clutched the porch where she sat, not looking at her brother. Her body slowly adjusted to the fact of the Archbuilder, its walking and speaking, scuffling in the dust, seemingly made of scraps, stage props, but alive, cocking its head curiously like an attentive dog, moving around the truck now beside the unconcerned men. She stared, perfectly still, fighting the urge to run. In one sense the Archbuilder was nothing, a joke, a tatter, too absurd to glance at twice. It seemed pathetic that they'd honored this thing with their endless talk, back in Brooklyn. That Caitlin had wasted her breath. At the same time, the Archbuilder burned a hole in the world, changed it utterly. It made the far-off towers loom up, made the glaring horizon draw closer. The place wasn't rubble everywhere. Somewhere there were more Archbuilders. The rubble and what grew in the rubble belonged to them. The girl felt her body understand.

The alien leaned against Ben Barth's truck, crossing its odd, double-jointed legs, watching as Clement and Ben Barth heaved a pallet of supplies from the back of the truck onto the porch. They'd driven the pallet from Southport, the older, bigger town, where there were doctors, stores, a restaurant, where people came and went. From what Pella had heard she already wished they lived there instead of here, in the new settlement without even a name, this place on the edge of nothing.

Ben Barth was shaped like a question mark, and he was a head shorter than Clement. But he looked like he belonged moving supplies off a truck, where Clement looked wrong.

"I'm sorry?" said Clement to Hiding Kneel.

"Misplaced intensity," repeated the Archbuilder.

"What's that supposed to mean?" said Ben Barth, with a hint of annoyance. He and Clement had one end of the pallet on the porch and were both behind it, pushing. Pella could hear the porch or the pallet splintering.

"The delivery could have been disassembled other-where," said Hiding Kneel, "and transferred in miniature. Rather than this present clunking challenge."

"Be less of a *clunking challenge* if you were helping instead of watching," said Ben Barth. He laughed sourly, and said to Clement: "Yeah, that's just how an Archbuilder would do it. Open a crate in the middle of the valley and walk each item back separately. Only they'd get so fascinated with the first one that they'd forget the rest and leave it out there."

Clement and Ben Barth got the pallet onto the porch. Clement stepped back and mopped his forehead with his sleeve. Ben Barth examined the crushed edge of the porch.

"Sorry about that," he said. "This wood is shit."

"Mangled surfaces," said Hiding Kneel.

"Yeah, mangled goddamn surfaces," said Ben Barth. "If you have to give every goddamn thing a name."

"Mangled surfaces is not a name, Ben," said the Archbuilder innocently.

"Neither is Hiding Kneel," said Ben Barth. He scratched at the sides of his grizzled beard. "But seems to me I know a somebody, or something, that calls itself that. So why not Mangled Surfaces?"

Pella was able to tear her gaze from the Archbuilder now. She sat staring past the house, to where the distant shapes met the sky, and thought: The whole *planet* should be named Mangled Surfaces.

"Come inside for a drink?" said Clement. "Ben? Hiding Kneel?"

Ben Barth nodded, and looked at the Archbuilder. "Sure," said Ben Barth.

"Why is your name Hiding Kneel?" said Raymond, following them into the house. Pella went too, feeling protective. It was one thing to meet Archbuilders outside, another to have them in the house. The four rough rooms had been divided now: the boys' bedroom, Pella's, one for Clement that was also an office, though it wasn't clear why it should be one, and the kitchen, where they ate. And hosted Archbuilders, apparently. Clement went to the refrigerator and began pouring drinks.

Ben Barth answered. "They're so in love with English, they had to go rename themselves that way. Truth Renowned, Rock Friend, Lonely Candybar, Hiding

Kneel. You'll meet the whole bunch, one name stupider than the other."

"Stupider and more carnivalesque," said Hiding Kneel, seemingly taking it as a compliment.

"Yeah, life's a carnival on the Planet of the Archbuilders," said Ben Barth. "Oh, thank you, Mr. Marsh." He took the glass of reconstituted juice.

"Call me Clement. This is Pella, and Raymond."

"Your name evokes," said Hiding Kneel, turning to Pella. "Pella Marsh."

"Evokes what?" said Pella. "I didn't pick it myself, anyway." She was distracted, noticing household deer scurrying around the edges of the room, finding vantage points. Little giraffe spies, everywhere.

The day before, the household deer had seemed new and strange. Now, compared to the Archbuilder, they were familiar and ambient, like weather.

"Kneel just likes the sound of your name," said Ben Barth. "That's all it means to say."

Clement handed Hiding Kneel a glass of juice. The Archbuilder lifted it to its dark maw and took a sip.

"Where's David?" said Clement.

"He fell asleep," said Pella.

"Yeah, with his head on the table," said Ray. "We made him go to his room. But I'll wake him up— he'll want to see *this*." He jerked his head at the Archbuilder.

"Ray, Hiding Kneel is not a *this*."

"He'll want to meet Mr. Kneel, is what I mean."

"Nor a *mister,*" chortled Ben Barth.

Raymond stood openmouthed, struck dumb by this second correction.

"Go ahead," said Clement, nodding. "Wake him up."

While Raymond and Clement talked, Pella watched the Archbuilder step over to the table, dip two furry fingers into the jar, pluck out one of the swimming fish, and dump it into its glass of juice. Pella looked over at Clement and Ben Barth, but they hadn't seen. In a little panic, she looked back at Hiding Kneel. The Archbuilder blithely lifted the glass and gulped down the fish.

Bruce had said they didn't eat the fish. But this one did, apparently.

So Bruce couldn't be trusted to know the whole truth about Archbuilders. No one could, probably. If the fish in the jar weren't important, something else would be, and she would have to learn that something else on her own. No one could be counted on to tell her. She felt the burden of this lonely knowledge fall on her, instantly.

She hoped David hadn't named his new pets. Or counted them.

"Kneel, are you listening?" said Ben Barth.

"Assuming the Marshes to be residing long and unveiling interest to me slowly, I wasn't, no," said Hiding Kneel. "Rather I was busily savoring nuances, details such as the name of Pella Marsh."

"Enough about that," said Pella. She disliked the way her name had gotten roped together with swallowing live things as *savoring nuances*.

"Well, get over here," said Ben Barth. "Mr. Marsh

isn't just any new homesteader on your dirty old planet."

"In as how?" said the Archbuilder, sidling toward them.

"In as he's an important politician from Earth," said Ben. "He's here to scrape us up into some kind of society. Be the first real civilization on this planet since your great-great-grand-whatever and their pals built those arches."

"Ah. What will you build?" said Hiding Kneel.

"Sorry?" said Clement.

"Whatever it is, it won't all fall down," said Ben Barth. "Isn't that right, Mr. Marsh?"

"Well, we're not building anything right now," said Clement. "I mean, besides a home. What I did back on Earth might be relevant at some time in the future; I'll do that kind of work if there's a call for it. But a planet with less than two hundred people on it doesn't have any use for a politician. I'm just here to join the community."

"Listen to him, Kneel. A speech maker, whether he means to or not. Now you're going to hear some English spoken around here, instead of that bunk of yours."

"I'm in a state of anticipation, anticipating statehood," said Hiding Kneel.

Raymond and David came out of the back, David rubbing his mouth and nose with a curled finger. "There," said Raymond, pointing at the Archbuilder, and whispering menacingly in his brother's ear. "Its name is Hiding Kneel. It talks crazy. And that guy is Ben Barth. He helped Clement with our stuff."

Pella caught sight of the household deer again, more than she'd ever seen before, all darting to take up positions around the room.

David stopped when he saw the Archbuilder, and stared. Hiding Kneel raised its glass of juice in a salute. Pella could only think of the potato fish that had been swimming in it a moment before.

David's face warped in dreadful slow-motion. The actual crying, the noise and tears, always waited until his face made itself ready. Like seeing a dish slip and fall toward the floor, it was impossible to do anything but watch.

Then it came, a roar of weeping. "The kid's scared," said Ben Barth delightedly. "He thinks he's having a nightmare, Kneel!"

"David, it's all right," said Clement. "Hiding Kneel is our friend." To the Archbuilder he said, "I'm sorry."

Raymond punched his brother lightly on the shoulder. "C'mon, David. Be brave like an arm."

David just stood and stared and cried. The situation freed Pella to study Hiding Kneel's face again, to stare down her own fear. To marvel at the furred, toothless hole of a mouth, at the burnished cheeks, the tangle of fleshy tendrils.

"We showed him *pictures*," said Ray, as though he were an old hand at Archbuilders, as though he'd seen more than pictures himself before Hiding Kneel appeared.

Ben Barth chuckled. "Pictures don't do that face justice, though, do they?"

"Could it be your countenance that has mispleased

the child?" said Hiding Kneel to Ben. "He had no similar photographic preparation for such an event."

"Get the big comedian, here," said Ben Barth. "You've really got to work on your delivery, Kneel."

Pella saw that Clement was paralyzed, made stupid by the situation. She went and plucked David away from his brother.

"Tell me what's the matter," she said.

"*What Raymond said,*" David howled.

"What did Raymond tell you?" Pella asked.

David controlled his crying enough to speak. "The potato fish were going to grow up into Archbuilders, like that one," he said, squeaking. "In the middle of the night. In the house."

"You know he's lying," said Pella. "I can tell you know."

David sniffed and nodded.

"The Archbuilders are okay," she said. "This one's a dork, anyway." She didn't care if Hiding Kneel heard. She couldn't be expected to go around protecting Archbuilders' feelings, on top of everything else.

"Raymond, don't confuse your brother," said Clement. "There's enough to get used to."

Hearing Clement talk in pallid euphemism, the very word *confuse* letting Raymond off the hook, made Pella yearn for Caitlin. She wouldn't have let the presence of an Archbuilder keep her from disciplining her children.

"You heard him, he knew I was kidding," said Raymond.

Pella kicked Raymond. Her contribution to his upbringing.

"There you go, kid," said Ben Barth to David. "Kneel's nothing to be afraid of. Archbuilders don't scare anyone for very long. I was just telling it how your dad is going to be running this place sooner or later. You're probably the most important family around here. The Archbuilders ought to be afraid of *you*, kid. Except they don't care."

"Nobody wants to do anything that conflicts with the Archbuilders," said Clement. "Quite the opposite—"

"I'm sure, I'm sure," said Ben. "Archbuilders aren't the problem. That's exactly what I was saying."

"We just want to live here, in a way that's in accord with the place." Pella could hear her father squirming, trying to slip off the podium Ben Barth was building for him. "Nothing needs running."

"See, *accord*," said Ben. He turned to the alien. "That's a word I can appreciate, Kneel. Used in its rightful place, not strewn around in any goddamn sentence."

The Archbuilder was moving toward the table again, its interest wandering. Pella walked quickly over, brushing past the Archbuilder, feeling its fur against her arm. She felt her face redden. Avoiding the Archbuilder's gaze, she picked up the jar of potato fish and handed it to David. "Put this in your room," she said. "It doesn't belong on the table."

"I should get going," said Ben Barth. "Come on, Kneel, give these people some time to get settled in here."

The Archbuilder turned, thoughtfully. It seemed oblivious to Pella. "My purpose is recalled," said the alien. "I wish to challenge you to a renewed tournament of backgammon, Ben."

"Not now," said Ben. "I've got to get the farm cleaned up. Efram's coming back in a day or two."

"Tonight will be fine—"

Ben winced. "You can't be coming around so much, Kneel. You know Efram doesn't want you around his place."

"Bruce Kincaid says Efram makes you work on his farm," said Raymond in one impetuous breath. "Why's that?"

"Who's Efram?" said Clement.

"He doesn't make me, kid," said Ben Barth.

"Why don't you have your own farm?" said Raymond.

"Because I wouldn't know what to do with my own farm, and because Efram needs someone to look after his, that's why."

"On your own farm backgammon could be played," said Hiding Kneel.

"That's enough out of you, Kneel," said Ben. "Come on, we're overstaying our welcome." He herded the Archbuilder toward the door. Pella saw household deer skittering out of their path. "See you, Mr. Marsh. You kids be good."

"Clement, call me Clement," said Clement. "Thanks for your help."

He waited a minute after they were gone, then said again, "Who's Efram?"

Pella and Raymond couldn't answer. They knew that Efram didn't like underground food, children who didn't take drugs to prevent Archbuilder viruses, or backgammon.

But they didn't know who he was.

The next morning they had another visitor, one as unsettling, in her way, as the Archbuilder. Tall, with her hair in a long ponytail, she might have been thirty-five. She was nothing like the other adults Pella had seen here, Bruce and Martha's parents, homely and suburban, or E. G. Wa and Ben Barth, the two gangly, stringy men, the stray dogs. This woman seemed to float above the surface of the planet slightly. She came in when Clement and Pella were cleaning up breakfast and looked at the new house as if she was appraising it for purchase.

"Diana Eastling," she said, and shook Clement's hand. "I've heard your name."

"This is my daughter, Pella," said Clement. Diana Eastling turned and nodded briefly. Clement said, "Will you sit for a minute? Have some tea?"

The woman nodded again, and went on looking hard at the house. Finally she said, "This is good. Yes. It's time for this."

"Time for what?" said Clement.

"Time for children here. You people with children will make yourselves a town. Tame the wilderness. It won't take much." She smiled at Clement oddly. And then she sat down.

"As opposed to some type of people who won't make a town?" said Clement. "I don't understand." He brought two cups to the table.

Pella followed him and took a seat at the table. Raymond and David were already out playing, led by Bruce Kincaid.

Diana Eastling smiled with her mouth closed. "I just think it's brave to come here with three children. And that it might actually lead somewhere, start a new chapter. I feel the same way about the Grants and Kincaids."

"I'll accept the compliment," said Clement. "Though I think it might have been braver, suicidally brave, to stay behind."

"I don't know about that, firsthand," said Diana Eastling. "I haven't been there for a long time."

"You've been here?"

"I'm a biologist," she said. "And I've become something of an expert in Archbuilder biology. I moved out here before there was any idea of a town. I suppose that's the distinction I was making before."

"Someone had to be first," said Clement, in a tone Pella hated. He sometimes sounded like he was awarding people a status they already possessed. "But you're glad there's going to be a town, I trust?"

"I don't care," said Diana Eastling flatly. "Anyway, don't credit me with being first."

The moment was awkward. Pella felt embarrassed to be at the table. She still hadn't uttered a word.

Like a household deer, she thought.

But Clement rolled on. "Maybe you'll feel differ-

73

ently when the place begins to take on some personality—"

"Well, I won't move away." Diana Eastling provided him another tight smile. "But then, I don't live that close now. Real towns have people like me living on their outskirts, if I remember correctly. That can be my contribution."

Clement nodded. Pella was aware of his desire to say the right thing to this oddly testy visitor. "It will take more than a few growing towns to ruin the solitude around here," he said carefully. "Big planet. Anyway, there's the Archbuilders."

"What about the Archbuilders?"

"If you never wanted to see a living soul—"

"Ah, yes. Archbuilders. Living souls. Indeed." She hesitated as if to laugh, but didn't. "Listen, when I said you were doing a brave thing, I meant one thing in particular: Your children aren't taking the antiviral medication. Or did I hear wrong?"

Clement barely paused. "You heard right."

"Well, I'm interested in that," she said cleanly. "I'll be very interested in the outcome."

Suddenly Pella felt the two adults not looking at her. Their not looking was tangible, an act.

"It's a part of taking the place seriously," said Clement. "Really being here. As far as I'm concerned. We can't just take pills forever."

We, thought Pella. Clement and his constituency, currently numbering three.

"Well, you've captured my interest, as I said." She got up. "Thanks for the tea."

Diana Eastling was good at keeping out of things. Pella wondered why she kept the skill so sharpened if she lived out at the edge of things, alone.

"Then I trust I'll see you again," said Clement. "That curiosity will draw you back to our place."

"I'm around."

"I'd like to know more about the Archbuilders. I don't get the feeling I'm going to learn much from Ben Barth."

"Ben Barth knows how to talk to them, which in a sense is everything. The things I know that he doesn't aren't very interesting to the layman."

"I'd rather be more than a layman," said Clement. "But you seem like you'd be a very impatient teacher."

"I wouldn't be any kind of teacher at all. I'm busy with my work. If urgent questions come up, I'll offer my help. I have a feeling I'll hear about it if they come up."

"From who? Ben's friend Efram?"

"It's not that big a planet."

"Can you tell me about Efram?"

"I'm not the best person to ask about that. Good day, Clement. Pella."

As Diana Eastling rose and moved to the door she turned her attention directly to Pella for the first time. Pella blinked and nodded. Diana Eastling's smile was actually pretty warm, but it still didn't draw her mouth open.

She seemed to have details like that well under control.

Six

Running, running—
  Watching:
  The girl woke from the odd dream.
  But she wasn't in her bed. She was out under the sky.
  And hadn't she, when she thought of it, been awake just now?
  The sky glowed gray and pink, and her old shock at its cavernousness came back to her. She turned her head, and an Archbuilder ruin, a column five stories tall, topped with a jagged overhanging beam, swung into view against the pink vault of sky. She was lying out in the rubble and vines; she felt them now against her back.
  She'd been out exploring, with the boy, the one her age. Bruce Kincaid. But she was alone now. Perhaps she'd gone off on her own. She couldn't remember.

Anyway, it was the middle of the day. She shouldn't be sleeping. She *hadn't* been.

Had she fallen?

Archbuilder ghosts whispered up the sides of the column. No, not ghosts. Household deer. They were everywhere in the fragmented monuments. The girl sat up, listened to the wind. She was alone, except for the glinting, invisible deer.

She thought of her mother, fallen in a seizure in the tub. Had Caitlin woken into a world as strange as this?

Was this what a seizure was, then? Dreaming awake?

Terrified, Pella stood up and ran stumbling over the flagstones out of the nest of towers, and right up to the edge of a sheer drop several times her height. She nearly plummeted, then righted herself, heart pounding.

She stepped back from the edge, looked down. It was a dry moat running as far as she could see, and it only got deeper farther on. Pella knew she must have come from the other direction. She looked up, but the sky was no help.

Five or six deer ran past her, giraffe necks bobbing, then plunged over the rim, a brakeless entourage. Lemmings, except they skidded and danced down the precipice, unharmed. She watched them flit away into the valley, until they vanished into the crystalline haze of sunlight on rock.

She turned and headed the other way, skirting the

shelf under the tower where she'd found herself just now, woken fallen and dreaming. She picked her way to a clear outcropping past the group of towers and, looking out, saw a building she thought was E. G. Wa's shop. Bruce Kincaid was nowhere to be seen.

She ran again, down the crumbled slope, into the valley. Wa's shop disappeared from sight again, but it didn't matter. She knew where she was. Out on the flats she slowed to a jog, but still huffing, panicked. Still no Bruce. She'd been here a week yet had never been alone, never been out in the open this long. Here, or back home, for that matter. Perhaps she hadn't woken from her waking dream. Maybe she'd failed to break the spell, her dream merely segueing into some more lucid phase.

But no, she was really here, running. Out on the mangled surfaces. Bruce had just gotten bored, and wandered off, probably. What needed explaining wasn't outside her, in the world or the situation. It was her state that was the puzzle. Her interior. Her lapse into— what?

She ran on.

She came across a gouge in the valley floor. Stones pried out of place, a patch of dust moistened into mud by what had been pulled out of the hole. Potatoes. It was a place where Bruce had been digging, she could tell. Such a sign of normalcy already, that she paused there, hopeful, fond.

She looked into the hole. Hacked-away vines trailed from the glistening gap, a socket like the space left when a baby tooth falls out. Bruce was probably cashing in the booty at Wa's shop.

Calmed somewhat, Pella trudged home.

Her house was in sight when suddenly she was not alone. A man in a hat stood on a ridge to her left, between her and the sun, so that he was a silhouette against the pink. Standing still, he was almost like another of the broken arches on the horizon, somehow drawn suddenly close.

She stopped, and they were both standing still. For a moment he just stared, one arm crossed over his middle, the other at his side, and Pella could imagine any expression on his face, and did. Then he started down the ridge toward her. She stood and waited.

"You headed up to that house there?" he said when he got to her. He pointed first at her and then at her house, in a gesture gentler than his voice.

She nodded.

"New family," he said. He was tall, but not spindly like E. G. Wa. Without his being at all fat, his hips were wider than his shoulders.

She nodded again.

"Well, I'm headed there myself. Ben told me, and I thought I'd come say hello. Only Ben must have left out that Marsh was remarried. You're too young to have had three kids."

Pella was bewildered, then astonished, as she worked it out, the meaning of what he'd said. Was he joking? "I'm *one* of them," she blurted. "One of the three kids."

Pella was already feverish in her panic. Now she felt her face flush with shame.

But *he* wasn't embarrassed. "Then this Clement Marsh must be older than I understood. You're not much of a kid anymore."

"I'm thirteen."

If he was making fun of her he didn't give it away. "What's your name?"

"Pella."

"My name's Efram." He smiled, and she permitted herself a look up at his face, but the hat cast a block of shadow across his brow and nose. His smile was bigger on one side than the other, and he held it so that it seemed carved in rock, the way he'd stood still when she first saw him.

Then he pointed again at her house, and again the gesture was soft, like he was shaping the air with his hand. "I guess we're going the same way, Pella."

"Yes," she said, and nodded too. Suddenly she wanted to be back at the house, badly. Something was wrong with this meeting. Maybe it was the way they were out in the middle of the valley, without even a porch for context. It seemed mistakes of scale were possible in this alien landscape. Pella could be taken for somebody's wife. Her father's, specifically.

And Efram Nugent could seem too big, out here. She wanted him adjusted, made smaller.

So they turned and walked together toward her

house, but that seemed wrong somehow, too, the sudden implicit alliance, the way it was as though she was bringing him home. Efram just sauntered along beside her, unperturbed, so still even as he walked that she felt skittery, like a household deer veering dangerously near a human's steps.

They walked like this, in silence, the one solid and unhurried, the other dynamic, bright, unhinged. Their shadows pulsed out in front across the rocks, pointing the way. Even as the girl felt like a household deer herself the actual deer massed behind the rocks along the path, watching. They knew to avoid Efram Nugent. They'd learned.

She ran up the porch steps ahead of him, abruptly completing the dash for home that Efram's appearance had interrupted. "Clement?" She went into the back, looked in all three bedrooms, called his name again. "Hello?"

Nobody was there. The house was empty.

She went back to find Efram. He'd stopped on the porch. "Well?" he said, and spread his big hands.

"Clement's not home," she said. "Um, do you want something to drink?"

"No thanks." He paused. "You look like *you* need one, though. Why don't you sit down?"

She felt a strange panic that he might enter the house. "I'll be right back," she said. She went inside, and poured herself a glass of water from the well tap. As she took the first sip she closed her eyes. The water was cool and tasted a little of soil or rust. Her heart was still pounding, her body still recalling waking on the hill-side, jerking out of the dream. Efram had come along too soon. There hadn't been time to consider what had happened, to keep it from playing on her face.

When she went outside, Efram Nugent was just walking around the other side of the porch, assessing the house as if it had fallen from the sky.

"Hello," he said. "Feel better?"

"Uh-huh."

"Something happen out there?" His smile was challenging and sympathetic at once.

"No."

"What were you doing?"

"Just walking around."

"I saw you run off that hill." He indicated towers, and then a slope, with his hand. His gesture was so specific that Pella felt he still saw her route there, sketched in air.

"I like to run," she said, and drank her water, letting it dribble down her chin, not caring. Droplets rolled, coated by the dust at her feet.

"You didn't look like you were running for the pleasure of it."

"Hey, Pella!"

David walked up, with Morris Grant. They were each carrying sticks, resting them on their shoulders. Morris had a fraying comic book curled into his back pocket.

"That's Efram," said Morris to David.

"Hello, boys," said Efram.

"What are you doing?" said Morris Grant.

"Talking to this young lady here," said Efram. He gestured elegantly. Pella felt a shiver of excitement.

"That's my sister," piped David.

Morris tapped David lightly with his stick. "He *knows* that."

"We're hunting household deer," said David.

"David—" started Pella angrily.

"That's all right, they can't catch them," said Efram softly, to her alone. To them he said, "Mr. Wa giving you a bounty?"

"Nope," said Morris. "He doesn't care about anything he can't eat or sell, the dumb old Chinaman—"

"Watch the talk, Morris," said Efram. "That's out of line, and you know it."

Morris's unit of value was attention, unqualified, and he looked ecstatic to be rebuked so extensively by Efram. He writhed with pleasure as he corrected himself. "I just meant we're not working for Wa, not like Bruce. He spends all his time digging up potatoes 'cause Wa gives him a nickel—"

"Tell you what," interrupted Efram. "You two want to work for me?"

David widened his eyes and looked at Morris. Morris nodded at David and then at Efram.

"You want to hunt household deer, go up to my place. Don't kill them, just roust them out. Tell Ben I sent you. If I don't see any around there before I go to bed tonight, I'll give you each a dollar tomorrow. How's that sound?"

"Not kill them?" said Morris.

"Nope." Efram winked at Pella. "Just send them on

their way. Herd them up west, where Diana Eastling lives, and Hugh Merrow. They *like* having those things around."

"I like it too," volunteered David.

"I'd like to kill one," said Morris.

"Well, I don't want carnage all over my farm," said Efram. "Just chase them out."

"C'mon," said Morris. Howling out a sort of hunting call, he raised his stick and charged past the house. David ran after him, adding a high-pitched echo to Morris's battle cry.

And they were gone, screaming off into the valley. Pella watched them disappear in a cloud of kicked-up dust. As badly as she wanted to torture Morris Grant with his own stick, she wished she was with them, running away from the house. She didn't want to host Efram alone for a minute longer. The pressure of it had her wanting, for once, to lose herself among the children, not be taken for someone older.

Efram just stood, emanating silence.

"Why do they like them?" she said, trying to fill the vacuum.

"What's that?" said Efram.

"Diana Eastling and the other name you said. Why do they like household deer?"

"Hugh Merrow. He's a painter, lives out on the western end, off alone. You know Diana Eastling?"

"She came by to see Clement. Like you."

"She recognizes your dad's name. That's what brought her out." Efram seemed to be talking to himself. Then he smiled. "I'm just humoring the boys.

They won't be able to herd those deer to Merrow's place, or Diana Eastling's, or anywhere else. Like chasing grapes around a plate with a knife. But I'll give them each a dollar tomorrow anyway."

"But why do Diana Eastling and Hugh Merrow like them?"

"You hold on to your questions, don't you?" He squinted at her, smiling.

"I guess."

"Well, Eastling and Merrow, they've got different excuses. She's a scientist—she's *studying* this place. Merrow's a painter, an artist."

He seemed to think no further explanation was necessary.

"And why don't you?" she asked.

"I'm sure you'll find out about that," he said. "The question is what you'll do about it." He stepped off the porch, and stood with one arm crossed over, the way he had when he'd first appeared on the hill. "I'll see your dad another time, Pella."

"Find out about what?" She heard her words come out panicked. Suddenly he was leaving, teasing her with what he knew.

He smiled. "We'll talk later, Miss Marsh."

He raised his big hand and held it up, until she felt compelled to wave. Then he dropped his hand and turned. Pella felt the air go out of her. She watched him track off slowly into the valley, not in the direction the two boys had gone, but toward Wa's.

Was he glad the new family was here? Did he want there to be a real town?

Would he sit in a rocking chair and drink Wa's coffee?

Pella stood staring after him, thinking.

Five minutes later, Clement came back, riding a bicycle painstakingly over the cracked ground. It was as though he'd been hiding until Efram was gone.

"Where were you?" she said. "I was waiting—"

"Look what I bought, from Joe Kincaid." Clement dismounted and admired the bicycle like a Christmas present, stroking the handlebars, the fender. "Joe said it was just sitting around. Great way to get around here, very ecological. Needs air, though."

He leaned the bicycle against the porch and went past her into the house. Pella stared at the bicycle for a moment. She imagined slashing the tires.

Then she followed Clement in, marveling that traces of Efram's visit weren't somehow evident to him.

"Where have you been?" he asked, his back to her, as he sliced at a green potato. He'd been quick to learn to cook the Archbuilder food, and now it was all there was in the house. At dinners he exclaimed over Raymond's and David's reluctance to eat it, as if it were burgers and fries, or chocolate-chip cookies, something he and they had been eating for a lifetime.

Pella found she couldn't answer the question.

Chop, chop. "Joe and I were talking about pooling together for some kind of school. They've been teaching Bruce and Martha at home, on Joe's computer. But now that we're here—and more kids will be coming. We're raising the new house tomorrow. Joe says the digging machine's almost finished the well—"

Then he noticed her silence. "Is something the matter?"

She looked at him helplessly. The question was inadequate. "I was just waiting for you and you weren't here," she gasped out in frustration.

Clement put down the knife and the potato he was holding. "What's wrong?"

What was wrong? There was nothing she could say. Not without saying that Efram had been at their house. And that would take explaining who Efram was. Which she didn't know. Anyway, describing what was so disturbing about meeting Efram would mean speaking of her waking dream, her trance, out among the towers. The two went together. And neither half of the story fit in words.

If she closed her eyes she might still be on that hill.

She found that she wanted to protect Clement from the fact of Efram's visit. *Clement never had to know,* she thought crazily, never even had to meet Efram—

But no, she realized, David had come by, with Morris Grant. He'd seen Pella talking to Efram on the porch, and then had gone off to Efram's farm. He might even see Efram again before he came home. And then he would mention it, innocently, to Clement. At the dinner table.

Anyway, Efram had meant to meet Clement. He'd surely succeed soon. The town wasn't that big.

Pella felt disastrous, compromised.

The thing she was hiding: if only she knew what it was.

But nobody had seen her out among the arches, not David, not Efram Nugent. Nobody knew about her strangeness, her visionary seizure, her dream. That was her secret with herself, a secret she might even be able to keep from herself. It wasn't part of any other story, was it?

"Pella?"

She moved toward her father, slowly, giving him time to catch the hint. He sat just in time, and she climbed into his lap. She didn't really fit there, but she drew up her knees and pretended. It was strange how Efram had mistaken her for a grown woman even as he towered over her, made her feel small. Whereas Clement, with whom she was still unquestionably a child, was nearly her same size. She might have been trying to sit in Raymond's lap.

The tears came so steadily and simply that she almost felt they were another kind of lie she had decided to tell about her impossible self on this least simple of days. It didn't keep her from crying them anyway.

Seven

Their first stop was the site of the new house. They snuck up. The girl didn't object to the childishness of it. For the moment she wanted to be lost in childishness, in her own ebbing childhood. So she followed Bruce Kincaid, the exploring boy, the leading boy. He guided the group of children up a ridge, an embankment of crumbled Archbuilder architecture laced with potato vines. Moving in quiet unison, they crept to the edge and peered over at the site. Viewed from above, as their shadows merged on the bleached rock, they might have appeared as a single six-legged creature, crawling with brilliant coordination.

The new homestead was a staked-out portion of the valley, the same as all the others. The girl wondered how the men chose where to put the homes, this one, or the one before, where she and her brothers and father lived now. Arbitrary, but then so was the town. The

planet, if you thought about it hard enough. The girl
tried not to.

The shape of the house-to-be was marked on the ground
by the largest pieces, the beams, the unraised skeleton.
Stacked in neat piles at the edges of the site were prefabricated panels, wallboard and flooring, hardware,
plumbing, and disassembled furniture, all of it driven
out from Southport on the back of Ben Barth's truck
and made ready for this day. The new place would be
identical to all their houses, that was obvious, even seeing it in pieces. It waited only to be buckled and bolted
together.

Clement stood below, with Joe Kincaid, and Morris's father, Snider Grant, and Ben Barth, and Hiding
Kneel. They were oblivious to the group of children
poised above them, watching from the ridge. They stood
squinting in the sun amidst the splayed panels and
beams, a puzzle in two dimensions that had to be assembled into three. Ben Barth was the leader. He spoke in a
low voice, and the other men, the fathers, listened. Pella
imagined Ben Barth and his Archbuilder putting up the
first of the homes, before any of the families had come.
Or had Efram helped, then? What about Diana
Eastling? Now it was the fathers, the family men, paving
the way for the next family, and Ben was the odd one in
the group, the bachelor. He and Hiding Kneel.

"New people coming," whispered Bruce Kincaid,
turning to Pella and the other children.

"Yeah, lesbians," said Morris Grant, louder.

"Shut up," hissed Bruce.

"Fuck you," said Morris. "They are lesbians. My brother told me."

"Yeah, well your parents are drunks," said Bruce. "Look at your dad—he can't lift a piece of wood. He should've stayed home."

It was true. Snider Grant staggered. He looked like he could barely stand the sunlight.

"Shut up, you fucker," said Morris.

Bruce turned and in one smooth, fierce motion shoved Morris down the embankment, away from the men and the house, out of earshot.

Morris slid downhill in the dust, teetering, as if in emulation of his father. But he stayed on his feet. When he skidded to a stop Bruce went and stood over him.

Pella and Raymond turned to watch. David and Martha Kincaid, less interested, remained at the edge, peering intently at the men below.

"It's true!" said Morris. "I swear. Doug heard it from Ben Barth."

"So what, why do you have to say it like that? Nobody cares."

"Lesbians, lesbians, lesbians," said Morris defiantly, even as he squirmed in retreat from Bruce.

"Shut up." Bruce advanced on Morris. Pella was surprised by his ferocity.

"I can say *lesbian* if I want," said Morris.

"Just ignore him," said Pella.

"What are lesbians?" said Raymond to Pella. He asked it earnestly.

"I'll tell you later," she said. Saying it, she reminded herself of Efram, of his warning that she'd learn about the household deer, his promise that they'd talk about it later.

The Planet of Withheld Explanations.

"Let's go," Bruce said to David and Martha, ignoring Morris suddenly, averting his eyes. "C'mon."

"I want to watch them make the house," said David hopefully.

"It's boring," said Bruce. "Takes forever."

So the group trudged away silently, their presence undetected by the men below. Bruce led them out to the west end of the valley, the direction, Pella knew, of Efram Nugent's farm. Morris righted himself and followed. No one objected. The group of six children had an awkward integrity, a completeness by now. Even Morris belonged in his place at the rear, scapegoat, outcast.

Bruce pointed at the house below the next ridge and said, "Hugh Merrow."

Morris Grant giggled. While they stood watching, a lone household deer skimmed past them, over the ridge, toward Hugh Merrow's house.

"He keeps to himself," said Bruce, in his adult-quoting voice. Then, more conspiratorial, "But Martha got in there once. He was going to paint her."

"Yeah, but I couldn't sit still," said Martha. She sounded pleased with herself.

"It's all full of paintings of Archbuilders," said

Bruce. "He loves to paint them. Guess *they* can sit still. Plenty of time on their hands."

The thought of Archbuilders and their time and their hands quieted the group.

"Let's go," said Bruce after a minute.

They took up another of their outposts, this time in view of Diana Eastling's house. They were making a kind of survey of the outer valley now, the zone of the solitary adults, the ones on the edge of the town, outside the world of families. Clearly it was also a spying mission, carried on in secret, even if it had never been declared one. They didn't mean to be found out. No sooner had Pella thought this, however, and they were discovered, caught off guard. Diana Eastling came up the hill behind them, out of the blinding sun, not from the direction of her house at all. It was as though she'd set a trap for them.

"Hello," she said when she saw them. She wore a big hat, like Efram Nugent's, and carried a shoulder bag.

Nobody returned the greeting. Diana Eastling didn't seem to notice. "You're Clement Marsh's boys," she said, nodding at Raymond and David.

"Yeah," said Raymond.

Pella wanted to speak, but couldn't. Just as she would have preferred to have the other children around her when she bumped into Efram, she would have liked to be alone now. Diana Eastling drew some feeling out of her that she couldn't identify. Diana Eastling's manner seemed civil and earthly, a relief from the fathers and the other men and the Archbuilders, from the grim and dusty feelings they inspired in Pella.

And Diana Eastling knew to be impressed with who Clement was, before. As impatient as Pella could be with Clement's political self, he'd at least been important. Here Clement seemed to be blithely willing himself into the dusty anonymity, gathering potatoes, riding bicycles, building houses.

"Carry on, scouts," said Diana Eastling, almost laughing. Her eyes were bright. "Go on with what you were doing. I didn't mean to surprise you."

Pella opened her mouth again, but nothing came out.

Diana Eastling turned, smiling, and went down toward her house.

Bruce led them through a pass that looped back east, and north. They fell into a line in the narrow gap between two hills clustered with fallen architecture, and one miniature arch that was a throwback, a living memory. Whole, unruined, it almost seemed to sing in the open air. Pella stared at it until she couldn't stand to anymore.

On the rise they caught a brief glimpse of Efram's farm, then it disappeared as they followed the dipping path. Efram didn't live so far away. The houses out in this direction weren't any farther apart than those the three families lived in. It was as wrong to consider the place Efram and Diana Eastling and Hugh Merrow lived the outskirts as it was to call the houses to the east a town. They were each only clusters of crumbs on a vast plate.

The only real difference Pella could see was the presence of the children themselves.

"I'm thirsty," said Martha, lagging, scraping her feet expressively.

"If you drink you'll just have to pee more," said Bruce.

"I'm still thirsty anyway," said Martha.

"We'll get something. Maybe at Efram's."

"Let's be in bed, let's be in bed," chanted Morris Grant from the rear of the line. He slurred the *t*, and ran the words together.

Bruce turned and glared at him.

"Let's all be in the lesbian bed," Morris went on tauntingly.

Then they turned a corner, and the view opened before them. A spread of enormous ruins, shapes Pella hadn't seen before, including another intact arch, huge, that framed a lopsided heart-shaped chunk of sky. And below, almost directly beneath them, was Efram Nugent's place.

The house was made of the same prefabricated panels, but that was the only resemblance. Attached was a greenhouse, a miracle of sparkling glass, a palace. The porch of the house was enclosed by screen, and the path through the compound was laid with gigantic flat stones, arranged like a solved puzzle. The buildings were surrounded on every side by a chaos of planting boxes, holding plants big and small, each protected by a sprawling canopy of wire mesh. Behind the house sat a chicken coop, full of brown hens, and a pair of metal tanks, which looked like they'd been salvaged from a crashed airplane. One of them had a hole punched in the top, rending the metal, and from it issued a steady stream of gray smoke. A few yards from the house stood a broken-down shed, the oldest-looking human thing Pella had seen on the Planet of the Archbuilders. Encircling it all was a crooked wire fence. Other homes clung to the floor of the valley like shells on a beach; this farm carved out a portion of the planet.

"Seems like a lot of work, just not to eat potatoes," said Raymond.

"He buys supplies, too," said Bruce. "He'd starve if he only ate what he grew. And Ben Barth takes care of a lot of stuff. Those are Ben's chickens."

"Me and Morris went down there yesterday," said David, pointing. "We didn't come this way, though."

"You scare away the deer?" said Pella.

"We tried," said David.

"Probably all came back five minutes later," said Morris. "We should of killed them."

"You can't catch them," said Bruce. "So don't even start talking about killing them."

"I did, once," said Morris.

"You're a liar, Morris," Martha shot out. She looked to Bruce for support.

"Well, did you get your dollar?" said Pella. "He should give you a dollar either way. You did the work."

David shook his head.

"Let's be in bed, let's be in bed," said Morris, under his breath.

"Quit," said Raymond.

"He promised you a dollar?" said Bruce. "You should go get it. Efram wouldn't cheat you."

"He said only if they were gone," said Morris, interrupting his chant.

"He'll give it to you," said Bruce to David, ignoring Morris. "Want to go ask?"

"He gave it to me, already," said Morris. "He gave me both of our dollars."

"That's a lie," said Bruce. "If anyone gave you two dollars you'd be at Wa's in a minute. You'd have candy smeared all over your face by now."

"Go ahead and ask Efram," said Morris. "He's probably not home anyway."

"Okay, and if you're lying I get to keep your dollar, right?"

Morris fell silent, instantly incriminating himself.

"You jerk," said Bruce, shaking his head. "Come on," he said to David. "Let's get your money. And Martha can get some water to drink. Even if he's not home."

"I'm thirsty for lemonade, not water," said Martha.

"You and Ray can see the place," Bruce went on, looking at Pella. "Let's go." He included everyone except Morris.

But Pella didn't want to go. She didn't want to see Efram, didn't even want to see his place. She ached to be away from the group, away from her brothers, away from Bruce Kincaid's demanding attentions. "You go," she said. She tapped Raymond's shoulder. "Watch David."

"David doesn't need anyone to watch him," said Morris Grant, asserting himself, desperately. "He was there with *me* yesterday. Ray wasn't even there."

"Get out of here," said Bruce. "You can't come with us."

"Don't tell me what to do." Morris panted. Again, he seemed weirdly happy to be attacked.

Pella could feel how it was this perverse delight of Morris's that got under Bruce's skin especially.

"I'm just telling you to get lost," said Bruce, his tone annoyed and pedantic. "You can do whatever you want after that."

Morris started for the path down the bluff, toward Efram Nugent's farm. Bruce reached out and caught his shoulders and pushed him down to one side of the path, hard enough that he toppled backward and landed on his open hands, then slid in the rubble.

As he came to rest Morris Grant began weeping. Bruce frowned at him. The other children stood in silence, waiting.

It was Raymond who finally spoke. "Where are you going?" he said to Pella.

There was a quiet complicity to his changing the subject, ignoring the noise Morris was making. The group was sealing up again, with Morris on the outside this time.

"I don't know," said Pella. "I'll see you later."

Bruce had already started down the steep path. Raymond half-ran to catch up with him. Martha looked back at Pella, quick and wide-eyed, then down at Morris in his dust and tears. Then she too ran to catch up with Bruce.

David marched after them, singing softly to himself, "Lesbian bed, lesbian bed—" The syllables were tentative, over-precise. The words meant nothing to him.

Then the group was over the crest, and Pella and Morris were alone.

Morris stood, crying quietly, undemonstratively now, his attacker and audience gone. He examined his palms, which were pink from their slap against the rocks.

"You okay?" said Pella.

"Don't baby me," said Morris, sniffling angrily.

"Okay. *God.*" Pella wanted to leave him there. She'd wanted to be alone anyway.

"Bruce is in love with you," said Morris sneeringly.

"Is not." Then, hearing her own response come out so petulant, she added, "That's ridiculous."

"He is so," said Morris, gathering steam. "He only hit me because he's trying to look big. He's showing off for you."

"He didn't hit you."

Pella regretted that, too, the moment it was out. She didn't mean to defend the brutal shove. That was Morris Grant's power, seemingly. He could make you regret anything you said to him. And say things you regretted.

"Everybody's on his side," said Morris, looking at his hands again.

"Are you bleeding?"

"I said don't baby me." He was done crying, and the words were free of their mournful aspect. He was just spiteful, now. Pella felt she was paying, somehow, for giving him the cookie on the porch at Wa's.

"Whatever," said Pella.

"I'm gonna get him," said Morris, looking up angrily. "You can tell him, too. I don't care." That said, he turned and ran off in the direction they'd come, feet kicking frantically out to the sides, as though somebody was chasing him.

Pella watched him go, feeling an unaccustomed dislike.

Then she ran too, wanting to leave the spot.

She dashed toward a cluster of ruins, neither following Morris back the way they'd come nor taking the path down to Efram's, but instead forging a third direction. She set out over obstacles, refusing to run a path, wanting to go the way that wasn't any option at all. She didn't care to be choosing, just running. Her steps clattered on rubble, and she winced, wishing to be invisible and silent, wishing to be unknown. She didn't want to remind herself of Morris, running.

She didn't even want to remind herself of herself. Just nobody running nowhere, unseen. That would be fine.

But instead of silence and invisibility, her foot plunged into a gap in the rocks with a sickening liquid sound. She was jerked to the ground, falling forward on her palms just as Morris had fallen back on his. She collapsed there helpless, twisting around to accommodate her leg, still up to the knee in the crevice that had felled her.

Wrapping her smarting hands under her knee like a sling, she pulled her leg out of the hole. Her shin was bleeding, and her sneaker was wet. She moved her leg, turned her ankle in different directions. It wasn't broken. She held off tears.

She looked down into the opening. Her weight had ruptured several potatoes, including a fish. As she watched, the little glistening bodies slid to the edges of the crushed, oozing mass. Dust rained down from the crumbled edge of the hole and flecked the dark, moist membranes. She turned away.

Unexpectedly, she was glad to be stopped. Stilled. Her breath rasped in her own ears as she sat, peeling down her sock, wiping her blood away from her shin. Now that she was sitting she saw there was no need to run. It was enough just to be away from the other children, to be in a place by herself.

The bleeding stopped. She leaned her head back against the rocks there, and closed her eyes.

"They're putting up the new house today," said E. G. Wa, leaning over his counter.

"More customers, eh?" said Efram Nugent.

"More customs," said the Archbuilder who was sitting in the rocking chair behind them.

Efram pointed at a drink in a plastic bottle. "Give me one of those." He was leaning on the other side of the counter. Behind him sat the Archbuilder, rocking rather frantically, waving its fronds. Standing near the door was a teenager, who Pella recognized from his sullen features as Doug Grant, Morris's mysterious older brother. She might have even mistaken him for a grown man, if he hadn't been standing in the same room as Efram. He didn't hold up to that comparison.

Household deer stirred in the corners and dashed across the shelves all through the room. Pella spotted them more easily than ever before. They almost seemed bigger. Was the light in the room somehow different? Or were her eyes growing more accustomed to finding them?

"Here you are," said Wa, handing Efram the drink. "You want one, Doug?"

"Sure."

"Thought so. Put it to your dad's account?"

"No, I'll pay."

E. G. Wa didn't offer anything to Pella or the Archbuilder. Of course, Pella didn't have any money with her. How odd, she thought, to carry money here. It was like the men were playing a board game. Or playing *store*, just to humor Wa. They knew it wasn't worth anything here.

"Yeah, old Ben Barth is right. Soon this place'll be running with people," Wa mused. "People and Archbuilders, all mixed up together. Need organization—I guess that's what Marsh is here for."

Pella was surprised that they were talking about her father with her in the room.

She was even more surprised when Efram answered, "Marsh has got some things to learn around here before he does any organizing."

He said it very evenly, without looking at Pella. Nobody was looking at Pella. She watched them all, silently waiting. She wondered if they even knew she was in the room. She felt oddly incapable of speaking. Invisible.

"I hope Clement Marsh has got some things to learn around here," said the Archbuilder, still rocking unrestfully, "because I am hoping to do some learning."

Doug Grant stepped in front of the Archbuilder, cutting him out of the circle. His movements were impatient, jerky, sprung, almost as though he were struggling to free himself from a web. He said to Efram, eagerly, "I always thought you were going to be the one doing the *organizing*."

E. G. Wa leaned forward and smiled, as if he'd meant the conversation to take this turn.

But Efram said, "You're jumping the gun—a couple of women take a house and you think you've got a town. There's nothing to organize, unless you need someone to organize your wishful thinking for you. Hold on to the customers you've already got, Wa."

"Earth's getting real bad, Efram," said Wa. "People are coming."

"This place doesn't have much to recommend it," said Efram with a kind of satisfaction. He sipped and swallowed. "Those two women might not like it here, go back. *Marsh* might go back. Not everybody turns out to like breaking new ground. And *nobody's* seen as much of this place as I have, spent as much time with these fools—" He tipped his drink at the Archbuilder. "Hell, maybe *I'll* go back."

"You'll never go back," said Wa.

I will, thought Pella. First chance I get.

Efram turned, and looked at her for the first time, his gaze shockingly cold. Still nobody had spoken to her, used her name. Efram stared, made a face, and stepped toward her, and she found herself flinching.

"You ought to clear this place out sometimes, Wa," he said over his shoulder. "Or do you like these things staring at you all the time?"

And then he raised his hand and with a big easy motion swept Pella off the windowsill where she had been perched, and onto the floor. Her four tiny legs scrabbled for traction, and instinctively, she ran.

Not alone. Three others were with her.

Three other household deer.

That was what she was.

Efram kicked at them as they ducked around the side of the counter, moving swiftly together, easily avoiding his boot, Pella moving as agilely as the others.

Then she separated from the other three. They darted around the other side of the counter, to spy on Efram and Wa as they resumed their conversation, while Pella made a dash for the door. She slipped past Doug Grant's feet at the doorway, and ran across the porch.

Then out, into the valley, to find her other, more usual self.

"Hey, Pella."

It was Bruce. Pella sat up. She was sitting in a tangle of vines on a flat rock in the bright sun. Bruce and Raymond stood over her. David and Martha were a little farther off.

"What happened to your leg?"

"Nothing." Oozing blood had circled her ankle, then dried. She rubbed at the crusted stripe with her thumb. "I stepped on a potato hole."

"So why were you lying there like that?" said Raymond. He sounded more resentful than concerned.

Pella didn't exactly have an answer. "I was just lying down for a minute," she said. She recalled her fugue, her visit to Wa's store. Her dash back across the valley. No, she didn't exactly have an answer.

"Looked dead," said Raymond, turning away disgusted, as if Pella had failed in some responsibility to him and David, some promise that she wouldn't ever look dead.

Pella felt that in some way she *had* failed. She got up, dusted herself off.

Martha stood sipping from a plastic bottle. David stood beside her, watching Pella, attentive, his hands a little out from his sides. The way Pella imagined he had watched Caitlin lying helpless in her shower.

"Anybody down there?" she asked Bruce.

"Nope," said Bruce. "Efram must be out somewhere. Maybe he's up at Wa's. We got Martha something out of his fridge anyway."

Pella didn't say a word, just trudged back with them.

Eight

"Invite Diana Eastling over for dinner tonight."

Pella had located Clement out behind the house. He was tamping soil from a bag into a trench in the ground. She limped up, her ankle a bit weak after all. Raymond and David were playing inside the house. Bruce and Martha had wandered home.

Clement looked up at her, a smudge of soil across the top of his nose. He pursed his lips. "That's a pretty specific request," he said. "What if she's busy?"

"Try."

"May I ask what this is about?"

"Maybe she knows about the Archbuilder viruses, about what they do to people."

Now Clement looked concerned. Pella felt only annoyance. She wanted to bypass his useless, uninformed attention. "Is there something I should know about?" he asked. "Are you . . . already experiencing something unusual?"

109

"No," she said, certain she was lying, certain she wanted to be.

"So what's the sudden urgent need for information?" He grinned and shrugged at her, rubbing dirt off his hands.

"Don't you think—" She knew she was being impossible, unfair. She wanted him to help her without fathering her, without arousing those instincts. Still, she persisted. "Shouldn't we find out more about it, *before* something happens?"

"If you feel that way, that's reason enough." He'd caught her tone now. "I don't know Diana that well, Pella, but we can ask. Do you really want to talk with the boys there?"

"I don't know."

"They're liable to ask a lot of silly questions."

"I guess." She was surprised. Clement would treat her like an equal if she insisted. If that was what she wanted.

A good question.

"We'll go ourselves," said Clement. "Find out what there is to know. Then you and me can translate for the boys later."

After dinner they set out into the north of the valley as the sun went down. The fragmented arches were all black silhouettes, against a sky still pink and peach beyond the ruins. It felt wrong walking alone with her father. Pella could think of only two or three times before, in the days leading up to Caitlin's death. In hospital corridors.

Diana Eastling's house was lit, visible from a distance. They approached in silence, without discussion, without a plan. Deer footsteps whispered in the darkness on either side of their path. Pella wondered for a minute if she shouldn't have come alone. Too late. They stepped up onto the porch and Clement knocked on the door. Pella drew in her breath.

The door opened, but it wasn't Diana Eastling who opened it. Efram Nugent stood with one hand on his hip, his big shoulders filling the doorway.

"Hello," he said.

"We were looking for Diana Eastling," said Clement uncertainly.

"You're Clement Marsh?"

"Yes."

"Efram Nugent. Pleased to make your acquaintance." He stuck out his hand, and Clement took it. "Diana's headed out south of here for a few days. *In the field* is how she'd say it. She asked me to keep an eye on her place."

"Ah."

"Why don't you come in?"

Clement looked at Pella and shrugged. "Sure."

Pella followed her father inside, crushed. Why wasn't the house dark? How could they have happened to find Efram here? This was worse than merely not getting what she wanted. It seemed in some way the exact reverse.

Diana Eastling's house was discouraging. It was so underfurnished and perfunctory that she might have only just moved in. Cardboard boxes were stacked against two walls of the front room and under the dining table. It looked to Pella as if Diana Eastling lived elsewhere, and kept this house for storage or camouflage.

And Efram moved through it as casually as if he owned it. They had entered his space. Possibly any space he inhabited was his, the way he moved his shoulders to carve the air. "I've been wanting to talk to you, Marsh," he said. "We keep missing each other."

"We do? I hadn't noticed." Clement grinned, meaning it to be funny.

"Pella didn't tell you I came around?" Efram pointed at her, as if she were off somewhere in the distance.

"No, actually," said Clement. "Maybe she forgot."

"Maybe," said Efram, raising his eyebrows at Pella significantly.

Pella turned and looked out the window, back across the porch at the jagged black landscape they'd crossed coming here. The sky was dark now, too, the sun finished.

The lit house had been a trap for them, a trap she led Clement into.

"Here." Efram pulled out chairs for them, as though they all belonged there in Diana Eastling's house. Clement sat, but Pella took the long way around the table, pausing to examine Diana's desk, which was loaded with disordered papers, stopping to peek into the unlit kitchen. She imagined briefly that Efram was lying to them, and Diana was in the house somewhere, hiding, listening. She wished it were true.

There were no household deer visible, anywhere. Pella went and sat down at the table, as far from both Efram and Clement as possible.

Efram exhibited his uneven smile. "People have been trying to get it through my thick skull that your coming here means something, that it's some kind of defining moment around here." He tipped back in his chair and swung his legs up onto the table, then took a pipe and a lighter out of his pocket. Pella stared. Efram not only put his feet on Diana Eastling's table, he smoked in her house. She wished he would burn it down, so she and Clement could flee. "I've been laughing it off," Efram continued, "but now it occurs to me they may be right."

Clement shook his head. "I'm just one man and his family, here to start over, Mr. Nugent. We may be part of a trend, but we're only part of it." Clement's voice was testy, brittle.

"Call me Efram. And let me finish. I was going to say maybe we need a defining moment. This is going to be a town, maybe a big town. That's okay with me." He lit his pipe and puffed out white, aromatic smoke. "And you're a politician," he added. "You want to be involved. That's okay too."

"I've worked as a politician. Now I'm working as a homesteader. I'm beginning to wonder what it is that's *not* okay with you."

"You don't want to be seen as a carpetbagger."

Pella wanted to cover her ears. The world seemed to

have closed in around them there at the table, and the two voices flew at Pella from different directions: Efram's a low ambient insinuation that wanted to surround her, take over the world, and Clement's a tinny broadcast from too far away to matter, but too nagging to ignore.

"I don't want to *be* a carpetbagger. I want to be a part of the community here. A growing place, that's something entirely new to me. I want to learn."

"Learning is good," said Efram. He took his legs off the table, his pipe out of his mouth, and leaned forward to peer into the bowl of the pipe. When he spoke it was as if he were reading something from inside the bowl. "What if I told you I thought we *needed* some organization, a few rules around this place?"

"You're headed somewhere, Efram. I don't imagine you're a person who ordinarily beats around the bush, but you're doing it now."

"Pella's a lovely girl."

"You'll embarrass her."

Clement's words seemed to Pella the very definition of inadequate. She was past embarrassment.

Humming with obscure shame and dread was more like it.

"Then I'll switch the subject," said Efram. He turned the pipe around and pointed it at Clement. "I think we ought to draw a line around this town we're starting here, Marsh. Make it a *human* settlement, a place where kids are safe."

"You want to exclude the Archbuilders, is that it—"

"And I want Pella and her brothers to take those

pills." The words were so lazily formed it was almost possible to ignore how he'd interrupted Clement to say them.

"This planet belongs to the Archbuilders, Efram," said Clement, as though he couldn't begin to address Efram's suggestions directly.

"I'm just talking about moving them out of our settlement. They don't care. They've got plenty of other places to wander around. A whole ruined planet for them to gawk at and wonder what the hell happened to their civilization."

"If we become a little embattled preserve—"

"Maybe you'd rather we become *Archbuilders.*"

"That's ridiculous."

Efram put his pipe in his mouth and pointed his thumb at Pella. "That's what you're doing to Pella if you don't give her the medicine."

"I don't think medicine is the right word for it."

"Do you think it's right to put a political experiment ahead of your children's welfare?"

"Politics you believe in should be reflected in the choices you make for your family," said Clement, angry now. "There isn't any difference between the two. If there is, you're a hypocrite."

"You were a Democrat, right?" Efram pronounced it so it nearly rhymed with *hypocrite,* as if he thought that might have been what Clement really meant. "I thought your party was against screwing with human biology."

"Please. We're a long way from our own scientific fiascoes here. These viruses have been stable for centuries. The Archbuilders remade their world from the ground up. It's pointless to regard some of it as suspect, unnatural. If we're going to live here, breathe the air, we've certainly got to find out what the viruses do to us."

Pella heard her father as Caitlin must have heard him. His authentic principles, his rightness. Only his rightness seemed lost here. Hopeless. She'd made it hopeless, with the thing she was hiding from him.

"Do to her, you mean," said Efram.

"Nothing's happened to her," said Clement confidently.

"Is that right?" Efram turned to Pella and raised his eyebrows, smiled.

Pella stared back, her mouth opening to speak. But nothing emerged.

It was her lie to defend.

The thing had only happened once. Twice if she counted the dream. Maybe never again. *But what if she wanted the pills?* She felt a swell of panic. She could sneak the pills, take them without anyone knowing—

As harshly as she felt toward Clement, she didn't want him to be wrong and Efram right.

But Efram nodded at her as she sat and stared, as though he already had his answer, or was getting it now.

Then she blinked her eyes, and was out in the night, squatting low on the summit of a pillar, staring out at the valley, her tiny body twitching, humming with awareness. Below her spread a tangle of ruins, threaded with vines whose leaves shimmered in the gentle, invisible wind. Beyond the ruins lay a homestead, one light shining through the windows, and through the porch window Pella could see three people seated at a table, two men and a girl—

"No," she said.

She was back at the table.

"*No* what?" said Efram, squinting at her.

Pella touched her own arms, her legs, trying to believe in herself, in the presence of her body. She felt the small throb of pain in her ankle, smelled Efram's pipe. She was here. Not outside. Not watching herself through deer eyes.

"Nothing's happened to her," said Clement furiously. "We discussed it."

"You discussed it?" said Efram, completely unruffled. "What prompted that?"

"No," said Pella, finding her voice. "Nothing happened." She said it to push Efram away, if only for a moment, and to assert to herself that she was *here,* in her human body. That she wouldn't drift out into the night.

Was this how Caitlin felt after her operation? Half-present, half-gone?

If she let herself drift and wander would she find her mother, somewhere out in the moonless valley?

"Fair enough," said Efram. "We're all agreed that nothing should happen." He took his eyes off Pella at last, and turned back to Clement. "So why not take the step to ensure that it doesn't?"

117

Clement stood suddenly. "Why don't you leave that for me and Pella to decide," he said.

It occurred to her that she should rise now, follow Clement, show her belief in him, as if this were one of his podiums, or convention halls. But she didn't stand. She was unsure her legs would hold her. So she stayed at the table with Efram, trembling, paralyzed by her fear that Efram was holding back something terrible that she needed to know.

She'd lied to protect herself. But it had become a lie to protect her father.

She closed her tired eyes, but their two voices babbled on maniacally. The room was filling with words, with shattered inflexible sentences. Pella wanted to howl, or to disappear. Instead she huddled, listening. Efram said, "I don't know if you and your kids ought to decide something that matters to everyone here, the whole town."

"I can't imagine why you think it's so important," said Clement.

"What you can't imagine," Efram shot back, "is exactly the problem. Things you can't or haven't bothered to imagine about the Archbuilders, things I know."

"You like to deal in vague warnings," said Clement. "If you know something, let's have it. I don't think you do. If the result of the viruses were known, I'd have read about it."

"You really think it's that simple, don't you, Marsh? Read about a place, then go blundering in. The map and the territory are the same."

"Well, not in one regard. You and your high-handed warnings weren't on the map to this place."

"I'm not the only thing. Trust me."

Now that she'd been outside, Pella could hear the wind, a low, distinct whine that seemed to rise and fall with their voices.

"Let's make this simple," said Clement. "Emigration to the American sector of this planet is governed by a man named David Hardly out of an office in Washington D.C. I applied there, Efram, and I guess you did too. They didn't mention a requirement that my children take the antiviral drug, and they didn't say you'd be instructing me on my behavior when I arrived. Until someone explains otherwise I'll assume we're under Hardly's jurisdiction here."

She opened her eyes again. Efram was grinning around his pipe. *"Jurisdiction,"* he said. "Now you're talking like a politician. Making sense like one, too. Dave Hardly's never even been up here. I've been living here seven years, mostly alone. You decide who you want to listen to."

Clement went to the door. "Thanks. I'll do that." He held out his hand for Pella. She thought, He doesn't know the way back without me. He'll make his dramatic exit and wander lost, have to circle back and humiliate himself asking Efram for directions. He doesn't have any handlers here, to grab him by the elbow as he walks off the podium. He doesn't have Caitlin.

She got up from the table in a rush, went past him and out into the night, not taking his hand.

Nine

The Archbuilder sat on a high stool in front of a window, perfectly framed by the ruins in the distant background, the pink sky above. The alien's mouth was slightly open, a tufted gap in the fur, beneath huge black eyes and shiny black cheeks. Its arms were folded, not together, but each back on itself, wrist to shoulder, inside its rustling paper garment. Soft, double-jointed legs crossed each other twice, knee and ankle. They appeared almost braided. Fronds stirred, gently. Otherwise the alien was completely still, an ideal model.

Hugh Merrow's face was washed-out, blond beard and eyebrows fading to sallow flesh, his eyes pale blue, and sharp. His clothing was covered with wipes, little finger-smudges of color, but the canvas he worked on now was roughed in with black and white and shades of gray. No color. He stepped away from his easel, squinting in concentration and annoyance as he crossed the room toward the Archbuilder. Brush between his teeth, he reached out and gently rearranged the fronds on top of the Archbuilder's head. The alien sat patient and unmoving, comfortable, apparently, with Merrow's touch.

Lining the edges of the floor were canvases, many of them Archbuilder portraits, some finished, glossy and built-up with layers of paint, others only sketched, or rubbed out in some places and heavily worked in others. A few were overworked disasters, knobbed with encrusted brush strokes, gnarled with color. There were self-portraits, too, Hugh Merrow glaring from the canvases the way he glared now at his Archbuilder sitter. And landscapes, sketches of vine-strewn ruins, distant incomplete arches in pink haze.

Hugh Merrow moved his brush to the windowsill, then put his hands back into the mass of the Archbuilder's fronds. The alien moved slightly, breaking the pose. Neither spoke. Hugh Merrow leaned over the Archbuilder, as though the fronds were a bouquet of flowers he wanted to sniff. The Archbuilder turned slightly, paper clothes rustling. The brush, jostled, clattered to the floor.

Pella risked a dash across the open floor for a better view. This she hadn't seen before. She scampered out from behind the cabinet, then up under the shelter of a chair, feathery limbs scrabbling silently. A jacket covered the chair back. Pella darted up through the hanging sleeve and poked her head over the top of the collar.

Hugh Merrow's tongue extended from his mouth, to meet the end of one of the fronds that lay across the Archbuilder's forehead.

Pella suddenly didn't want to be seeing it. She tucked her head down, and clung there inside the coat, trembling, angry at Hugh Merrow for what he was doing in front of her, as though her presence were known to him.

Whatever he was doing, it wasn't painting. She knew that much.

She released her hold on the inside of the jacket, ran across the seat of the chair and onto the floor, moving to the window that was her way in and out of Hugh Merrow's place.

Then, changing her mind, she didn't bother escaping, just woke, allowed her perceiving self to flow back into her human body, where it lay, sleeping and hidden. The deer could find its own way out.

Back in her dark secret nook, she opened her eyes, her real eyes, and knew instantly that she wasn't alone.

When the Archbuilder virus infiltrated her body the girl felt an urgent need to search the hills and towers west of the settlement, to look for a hiding place, a burrow, a safe house for her human body, like a bird in spring compelled by instinct to build a nest. What she found was a chunk of fallen architecture with a half-collapsed chamber, a thing that might have been a turret, a tower room for a prisoner in a fairy tale, a kidnapped woman or a man with a scarred face. The girl pictured the fragment high on the arc of some gigantic buttress, but now it lay on its side in the seam of a gully, a spot sheltered from most views, and so dark and protected that

Archbuilder potatoes grew there, just inside the entrance, exposed to the open air. The fragment was the sort of archaeological clue that the girl imagined Diana Eastling was out combing the planet to find.

The girl cleaned out the vine, sold the potatoes to Wa, then kicked dust over the muddy traces of the potato nest. Even so, she huddled at the opposite end of the chamber, away from where the potatoes had grown. She had stocked her nook with three jars of water and a blanket, stolen from a supply pallet behind the Kincaids' house. Nothing else, no books, no paper, no games. The girl didn't read or play there, just closed her eyes and went away, into the body of a household deer. The hiding place didn't have to be anything more than what it was: secure, private. Though she wouldn't mind if it were warmer. Lying still for hours, the girl would wake shivering, even wrapped in the blanket.

The girl had snuck in to watch the painter and his Archbuilder models three times before. As she saw it, she was practicing, mastering her fear and awkwardness, learning what it meant to be a household deer, a spy. She didn't care what she saw when she practiced this new art; she was only finding out what was possible. She'd been in E. G. Wa's shop, seen him fussing and cleaning in the back, picking his nose, staring out the window as he waited for his nonexistent customers. She'd watched him go to the bathroom, elbows on his knobby knees as he sat. And she'd climbed into the cab of Ben Barth's truck the day before, and ridden with him out to Efram Nugent's farm. She hadn't gone in, though, hadn't wanted to see Efram again, even nearly invisible, as she was. She hadn't forgotten the moment in Wa's shop, when Efram had seemed to see through her deer-self, to Pella. So she'd crept out of the truck and tiptoed through the maze of planting boxes in Efram's yard, then, suddenly spooked, had woken.

Once she'd crept around the edges of the Grants' house, but she didn't go in. She didn't want to see Snider and Laney Grant, the drunk couple who never left their house, didn't want to know what Morris Grant faced when he went home. She only waited on the porch awhile to see if Doug would come out. He didn't. The girl saw Doug Grant when she spied at Wa's, never anywhere near his parents' home.

Ben Barth, Hugh Merrow, E. G. Wa—these were the bachelors, the harmless ones, as Pella saw it. She allowed herself to practice on them. She didn't want to spy on the families, not even her own. She didn't want to see anything that mattered. She only wanted to amuse herself and explore the boundaries, the functions of the gift.

Someone knelt over her in the dark. Someone had found her in her hole. She blinked and worked out his silhouette in the light leaking through the entrance. Bruce Kincaid.

"Pella?"

Of course *he* would find her. The digger, the clamberer, the collector. She'd hidden where potatoes grew, so what did she expect? She should have built her hideaway in a closet in her house, right under Clement's nose—there she would have stayed undiscovered. It was Bruce Kincaid who'd been asking where she was disappearing to. Her father hadn't even noticed how much time she spent missing, hiding.

"Pella?"

"I'm here." She sat up. He couldn't see yet, she realized. The sky was bright and he was still blinded, coming into the dark turret.

"You didn't answer."

"I was hiding."

"I touched you, and you didn't say anything. I had to wake you up."

"Touched me where?"

"Your *arm,*" he said, exasperated.

"I didn't feel anything—"

"C'mon, Pella. You were asleep. Or out cold."

She turned, and moved closer to him, trying to find an angle in the dim light that allowed her to read his expression.

"What's going on?" he said.

She hesitated, then said, "Let's get out of here."

She nudged his arm, and he duckwalked back through the entrance. She followed, shucking off the blanket.

"You're leaving that in there?"

"Yeah. Shut up."

They climbed out of the gully together, silent. The sun was high, and their shadows were knotted at their feet.

"So if you weren't sleeping, what were you doing?" he asked finally.

"I *was* sleeping," she decided.

"This have anything to do with your not taking the pills?"

"I guess." She'd let him supply the explanations, believe what he wanted.

"What happens?"

"Nothing. I just need to sleep a lot."

"That's it?"

His plain disappointment made her almost want to tell him. "That's it," she said.

"Morris Grant said your mom had seizures," he said suddenly.

"What does Morris Grant know about it?"

"He said David told him."

"Just two," she said. "One at home, one in the hospital."

"This doesn't have anything to do with that, does it?"

"No." She refused the notion so firmly that only afterward did she realize she needed the clarification herself.

They were silent again for a while, climbing the ridge. The sky was peach-hued, awesome and empty, no variation to give it more than two dimensions, or fewer than a billion. The crunch of their alternating footsteps mimicked an echo. Smoke huffed up past the rise on their left, gray-pink against the hill, but nearly impossible to make out as it rose into the sky. It came from Efram's backyard kiln. Pella intentionally bumped against Bruce, steering them in the other direction.

"Maybe you're just sort of warming up for something," said Bruce as they walked along.

"What do you mean?"

"Like, your body's changing, because of the Archbuilder viruses. So that's why you need to sleep a lot."

"Maybe."

"What about Ray and Dave? Is anything like this happening to them?"

"Nope. And they don't know about it, either. You're going to keep quiet about this, right?"

"Sure, if that's what you want."

"Yes."

If he were one of her brothers she would have had to back it up with a threat of some sort. But Bruce Kincaid smiled, and she realized he wouldn't tell, simply because it made his life more interesting to have a secret with her.

She thought of what Morris had told her that day on the ridge over Efram's farm. That Bruce loved her. If it was true she didn't want to know about it, especially here, walking alone with him, indebted to him for protecting her secret, her hiding place. Let him keep both secrets, Pella thought. Mine and his own.

"And anything else," he said.

"What?"

"Anything else I can do," said Bruce. "To help you." He sounded annoyed, like she wasn't getting into the spirit of it.

"I can't think of anything." She wished she could

tell him that not talking about it included not talking to *her*.

"Maybe I'll stop taking the pills too," he said.

"Don't."

"Then whatever happens, happens to both of us—"

"Forget it, okay? You'll be glad. I wish I could forget it myself."

"So do you want me to get pills for you? I could."

Would she want to let go of her deer-self, so soon after discovering it? Stop sleeping, stop spying? Then she thought of Hugh Merrow, of what she hadn't wanted to see. The curtain that had parted. Maybe she did want to take the pills, after all.

"Wouldn't they notice them missing?" she said.

"Who?"

"Your parents."

At that moment a household deer ran skittering between them and sprang up onto a rock to the right of their path. Pella stared at the deer. It cocked its head at her questioningly.

Could someone be looking through its eyes?

"I'll steal them from Wa's," said Bruce. "He's got a shelf full of them."

If nothing else it would keep Bruce busy, divert his attention. "Okay," she said. "Do it."

They came to the ridge that overlooked the lesbians' house. Llana Richmond and Julie Concorse, and their baby, Melissa Richmond-Concorse. It was no longer remarkable. Six days before, Pella and Bruce and the other children had stood here and watched the men prepare to fit this house together. Now it was already lived in, a part of the town.

"I could find you a better hiding place, too," said Bruce. "I know lots."

"Who's going to find me where I was, except you? I bet you had to follow me, anyway."

"Well, yesterday I watched what direction you went."

"I knew it. I just hope Morris Grant wasn't following *you*. He's probably out there kicking in the sides of my thing, just to see if he can."

"He didn't follow me."

Julie Concorse came out onto the porch of the house below and dumped a plastic container of dirty water over the edge, without looking up and seeing them. The water made a dark spider-shaped stain on the rock in front of the house, topped with a lump of soap bubbles.

As she watched Julie Concorse disappear through the front door, Pella imagined herself in her other form, a household deer slipping inside the house.

"There was a couple like that living next door to us, in Bryn Mawr," said Bruce. "We shared an under-garden with them and some other families. Only they had a boy."

"A baby?"

"About Martha's age. It's kind of weird, lesbians and a *boy*."

"Doesn't matter," said Pella, squelching his enthusiasm.

The only way she knew to manage right now was to smooth down all irregularities, to placate Bruce and anyone else. Everything would be normal, everything would be okay. Nothing would be weird. She would keep weirdness contained within herself, to protect the others. Foremost among them, Clement.

They walked on until they stood in front of Pella's house. "Well," said Pella, wanting to be rid of him now.

"See you later, I guess," said Bruce.

"Okay."

"Let me know what's going on, okay?"

"Shut up, don't talk about it here."

"Sorry. Bye." He looked at her wanly, raised his hand, then headed off, half-running.

Raymond was in the biggest chair, with the album of family photographs spread open in his lap. Pella hadn't seen it since they'd packed it up, back on Pineapple Street, those last few days. Raymond looked up surprised, and snapped the album shut.

"What are you doing?" said Pella.

"Nothing."

"Where's Clement?"

"You know, with Joe Kincaid. Talking about the school thing."

"What about David?"

"I dunno. He and Morris and Martha were going around."

"Why didn't you go with them?"

"Didn't feel like it. Why didn't you?"

Pella didn't answer. Instead she went through to the bathroom and locked the door from inside. She pushed her pants to her ankles, plunked down on the toilet and peed. Finished, she hunched forward on her knees, eyes shut. She already wanted to silence her thoughts and wander again, from herself, from the trap of the family house. She couldn't bear to go back out and see Raymond huddled with the photographs, grown reflective at last, at the wrong time.

Craving distance, she let herself drift, sitting there with her chin on her crossed wrists. In a moment she woke into a lithe body running from under a monumental shadow, into a patch of sun. A household deer again. She scampered over a fallen pillar and back into shadow, and Hugh Merrow's house came into view.

Her curiosity had called her back here.

Around the corner, up the wall, and through the window, then down, on silent feet, into the room. Pella was nothing but eyes and feet now, the rest of her only a tremble in-between. It was easy to ignore a tremble, let eyes follow feet. She dashed up on a table and looked around.

The Archbuilder was gone. Hugh Merrow was at the sink, washing his brushes, scumbling in a jar of turpentine, then kneading the bristles back and forth against the porcelain. If something had gone on between Merrow and the alien, it was over. Pella had managed to miss it, exactly.

Whatever they'd done hadn't advanced Merrow's portrait of the Archbuilder. There wasn't any color rinsing out of the artist's brushes, and the canvas sat looking precisely as it had before, a sketch in gray wash. Unfinished, forgotten.

Ten

"Put the chairs in a circle."

"That's not like school."

"Are you complaining?"

"I thought you didn't want—"

"If we're gonna do it we should do it right."

"There's no right way. This is something different, as you'll see—"

"Chairs in a circle is different like *kindergarten.*"

"We could use the porch."

"No, then they'd just be distracted."

"We'll be distracted *inside,* watching household deer."

"I'll chase them out."

"No, Morris, set up the chairs."

"He wants to be deer monitor."

"That sounds like the name of an Archbuilder. Deer Monitor."

* * *

Clement had cleared out their living room for the class-room, the one-room schoolhouse. Joe Kincaid, who'd been a professor in Pennsylvania, was teacher, which made Clement what? The principal? The dean? The class consisted of Pella, Raymond and David, Bruce and Martha. Plus Morris Grant. And two Archbuilders. One was Ben Barth's friend, Hiding Kneel, the other the one Pella had seen at Hugh Merrow's, whose name was announced as Truth Renowned. But not Doug Grant, who at fifteen apparently judged himself too old, and not Melissa Richmond-Concorse, the lesbians' baby, who at two wasn't old enough.

On a high shelf in the corner perched two house-hold deer, waiting.

Only the Archbuilders were enthusiastic. The fathers strung along the children on the promise of something unusual, or there would have been outright rebellion. As it was, Joe Kincaid and Clement Marsh were meeting with passive resistance. If the families were laying ground for a new society, all the more crucial school be kept out of it. Why clean a slate only to make the same drab marks on it again? So the children dragged their feet, honorably, in the name of later generations, children who would view them as architects of a paradise.

Anyway, six children and two Archbuilders weren't a class, and two fathers weren't a school. The objections were endless. Yet here they were, seated in an abysmal circle, forced to stare at one another as they listened.

Outside, the irregular sun-splashed terrain of the valley beckoned. Being drawn indoors made the children feel they were creatures of the valley now, as much as the Archbuilders, maybe more.

Pella sat with her feet up on her chair, arms around her knees. She picked idly at the scab on her ankle, eyes focused through the window, on the distant horizon.

"—we're not going to pretend that you're all reading at the same level," Joe Kincaid was saying. "Or should be reading the same things—"

"We are all reading on the same planet," said Hiding Kneel, leaning forward into the circle. The two Archbuilders sat together, Hiding Kneel agitated, fronds in motion, Truth Renowned silent and shy, arms and legs tucked away. Though no one admitted to fear of the Archbuilders, the children had given them plenty of room.

Seated near the windows, their fur glowed in the sun, looked almost wet in shadow.

"Uh, yes," said Joe Kincaid. "I guess that's the point. One thing that's certain is we're on the same planet. Sharing what we learn about it is as important as any other sort of schoolwork. I know Bruce and Martha are studying at home, and I guess your mom gives you lessons at home too, Morris. Anyway, this will be the *opposite* of kindergarten, for whoever said that. We'll call ourselves a study group, which is a kind of school *I* didn't have until college. But I didn't live on another planet when I was growing up either."

"That suggests that you are not growing up now," said Hiding Kneel.

"Ah, good point. I should know better, since part of what I'm getting at is that you're never done learning. For instance, lots of Archbuilders speak English; Clement has decided to be the first human to speak Archbuilder—"

"There's no such thing as speaking Archbuilder," said Raymond. "There's hundreds of languages. Caitlin said. Remember?"

"Well, I'll study one of the languages," said Clement. "Our Archbuilder members here can help me decide which would be a good choice. Just listen to Joe for now, Ray."

Pella felt the scab on her ankle scratch off under her fingernail, then a little chill of pain where blood met open air. She cursed her body. She wanted to hide it away.

"We'll meet twice a week," Joe Kincaid went on. "I'm sure some of you will be quite relieved to hear that. This doesn't mean you can quit your independent-study work. What we'll do here is get together to talk about what we're learning. The older kids can help the younger ones with hard material, and native speakers can help students of new languages. Teaching is one of the best ways to learn."

"Sounds like college is dumber than kindergarten," said Morris Grant.

"Kindergarten didn't have Archbuilders," said Bruce.

"And Archbuilders didn't have kindergarten," snorted Morris.

"Rather, we have a system of tutorship—" began Hiding Kneel seriously.

"Maybe we'll bring in guests to speak to the group," said Clement, trying to reassert control. "Diana Eastling, if she could be convinced—"

"Let Hiding Kneel talk, Dad," said Raymond. "I mean, all Diana Eastling does is *study* the Archbuilders. Kneel *is* one."

Pella's attention quickened at the mention of Diana Eastling. As far as she knew the biologist was still away, exploring. Had Clement seen her?

The one place Pella wasn't spying was home. Who knew what Clement was up to?

Clement said, "Fair enough—"

"The germs of the word *kindergarten* elaborate certain paradoxes in our situation," said Hiding Kneel, fronds waving. "We are not young, nor do we generally produce offspring. Otherhandedly, we are all children of the generation that preceded us, those who reshaped our world and then abandoned us to it. Further, *garden* indicates a preserve, a cultivated portion, but there is none such. We meander in ruins and waste. Yet again, our providential potatoes grow ubiquitously, and the climate is like a—I cannot recall the word . . ."

"I don't know," said Clement, when no one else spoke. "I can't think of what word you're after."

"Don't start him up again," said Morris Grant. "He'll talk forever."

"A *hothouse*, thank you," continued Hiding Kneel, as though Morris or Clement had supplied the word.

"And so *kinder* in a *garden* is seemingly on-target. Begging the pardon of Morris Grant, I regard it flawed to say we don't have kindergarten. Indeed, we more lack anything other."

"What?" said Morris Grant.

"And your, uh, system of tutorship?" said Joe Kincaid.

The two household deer on the shelf in the corner were in motion, bouncing, shaking. Pella squinted to see better. One had mounted the other, was pumping frantically. Unmistakable. Like a nature show about mating bears or lizards. The one thing that was done the same everywhere.

Except by Archbuilders, thought Pella. They weren't split like all the rest of the world into fuckers and fuckees.

"Our system of sleeping and dreaming, you mean," said Hiding Kneel to Joe Kincaid.

"If that's what you mean—"

"Certainly," said Hiding Kneel. "I learned English that way."

"Hear that?" chortled Morris Grant. "It learned English asleep. No wonder."

"Shut up," said Bruce.

"Please, explain it to us," said Joe.

"Let Pella Marsh do that," said Hiding Kneel, uncurling its tendrils in her direction. "She may be better able."

"What?" said Pella, startled. She'd been staring at the humping deer, imagining herself displaced into one or the other of them.

"I suggest you might elaborate the method of education by reverie," said the Archbuilder.

Pella's face heated. "What makes you think I know anything about it?" she said fiercely.

Archbuilders sleeping, household deer creeping, and Archbuilders learning English asleep. Spying on people, that's what Hiding Kneel meant. Education by reverie. No wonder Efram didn't like household deer.

She'd take the pills, she decided.

"What's this, Pella?" said Clement.

"Nothing," said Pella, glaring at Hiding Kneel, ignoring Clement.

"This school is off to a great start," said Morris Grant, with heavy sardonic emphasis.

"I like it," said David sincerely.

"You said we were going to have snacks," said Martha Kincaid to her father.

"In a minute," said Joe Kincaid. "First let's pair off into study partners—"

Pella was matched with David. She turned her back to Clement, hoped he'd forget what Hiding Kneel had said. Morris Grant was paired with Clement, clearly by design. Hiding Kneel was Raymond's partner, and the other Archbuilder, Truth Renowned, was matched with Martha Kincaid.

"Might we now play backgammon?" said Hiding Kneel excitedly.

There were heavy footsteps on the porch.

* * *

They all turned as the door was thrown open. Standing like a statue in the sunlit doorway was Efram Nugent. He didn't step inside, but held there, silhouetted in the light, and surveyed the room, then raised his hand and pointed at Truth Renowned.

"Step away from that girl," he said.

Truth Renowned stood beside Martha Kincaid, fuzzy limbs folded together like braids, fronds wavering. No one spoke.

"You heard me," said Efram, the three words strung out like gunshots in the distance.

Household deer scooted through the doorway past Efram's feet and made for the dusty shadows.

Efram's presence was irrevocable. The day was smashed into another shape by his arrival, the air itself made watery. Pella felt a treacherous thrill seeing him wreck the classroom with his insinuations.

Truth Renowned, of course, couldn't look less dangerous.

"What is this?" said Clement. "What's going on?"

"We've been looking for this one," said Efram. "Should have figured it would take a chance like this to hide. Play school."

He moved into the room. Behind him, revealed in the doorway, stood Ben Barth and Doug Grant.

Now Clement stepped forward, out of the double row of study partners that stood frozen in the middle of the room.

"What are you talking about?" he said, his voice rising. Pella heard the tone that had cost him the election, the tone of the lost cause.

"It's not a thing that we'd want to talk about in front of all these kids," said Ben Barth. "Has to do with this Archbuilder, though, and Hugh Merrow. Not a pretty thing, Mr. Marsh."

Efram stared at the alien, ignoring Clement. "Truth Renowned knows what we're talking about—don't you?"

"I'm not sure," said Truth Renowned, revealing a voice at last: a warble, a quaver. "Hugh Merrow preferred that I not speak about these matters."

"Well I prefer that you do speak," said Efram, adding only after a pause, "about these *matters.*"

"Evidently conflictual!" said Hiding Kneel.

"Oh, oh—," said Truth Renowned.

"Not here, Truth," said Efram. "Outside." He pointed at the door.

"Truth Renowned is a guest in my house," said Clement, stammering. "He—*it,* I mean, can stay as long as it likes."

"I wish to depart," said Truth Renowned.

"You mean you want to go with them?" said Clement.

"I think I would prefer not to do that," said Truth Renowned weakly.

"Enough," said Efram. "Let's go." He pushed Truth Renowned roughly on the shoulder, and the Archbuilder stumbled to the door. Doug Grant moved out of the doorway, a twisted expression on his face, and grabbed Truth Renowned's arm as the Archbuilder passed.

Efram took Truth Renowned's other arm, and together they steered the alien across the porch and down the steps. Clement rushed after them, but Ben Barth put his hand out and caught Clement's shoulder. "Slow down, Mr. Marsh. Efram knows what he's doing."

"That's what I'm afraid of," said Clement.

"Be patient, Clement," said Ben Barth. "Let Efram get his information straight, so we'll know what's called for."

Clement lifted Ben Barth's hand and went past. Joe Kincaid followed, and so did Hiding Kneel. The children trailed after them, onto the porch, into the sun. Pella was grateful to Efram for dragging them out of the cloistered schoolroom, into the day. No matter how he had to do it.

Her fear of the sky was gone. Now she only wanted to be a thing out in the valley, running.

Efram and Doug Grant pushed Truth Renowned ahead of them on the path from Pella's house, in the direction of Hugh Merrow's. They let go of the alien's arms and the Archbuilder trudged along, acquiescent.

Clement rushed after. "What are you doing?" he demanded again.

"I want Merrow to look his friend here in the face," said Efram. "See what they have to say when they're both at the scene of the crime." He turned back to Clement, putting his hands on his hips. "Come ahead if you want," he said, and grinned to mark the challenge. "You probably ought to be there." He gave Truth Renowned another shove, just for show.

Clement was defeated. If he followed it was as if he'd taken part in the posse. He followed anyway. Joe Kincaid jogged along sheepishly behind him.

Morris Grant jumped down off the porch, ran out and fell into step beside his brother, as the captive Archbuilder was led over the ridge.

Ben Barth turned to Hiding Kneel. "C'mon, Kneel," he said. "You can help your friend find his tongue. Figure talking's the one thing you know something about."

Hiding Kneel shuffled down the porch steps after him, silent for the moment.

"Let's go," whispered Bruce to Pella.

Pella couldn't think. The men and Archbuilders were disappearing into the valley, behind the cloud of dust raised by their scuffing steps. Rushing off to make their disaster. Pella felt she had to witness it. But not with Bruce. She would have preferred to follow invisible, as a household deer.

"Someone has to take care of Martha," she pointed out.

"She can stay here with Ray and Dave," said Bruce.

"I want to go," said Raymond.

"You have to watch David," said Pella to her brother. "And Martha too. Get her a snack."

Eleven

Hugh Merrow had been drinking. His house was like a tableau arranged to produce that impression, littered with bottles and glasses and laundry, shades pulled down against the light, a twice-bitten sandwich rotting on a plate, and the artist himself slumped in a chair in the center of the room, his forehead braced against his palms. The easel was empty, the sketch for the portrait of Truth Renowned down, facing the wall. The self-portraits on the walls glared into the middle of the room accusingly now, and the rosy landscapes seemed to mock the sealed windows.

The painter barely looked up as they came in. First Truth Renowned, pushed ahead roughly by Efram and Doug Grant, then Clement and Joe Kincaid. Next, trickling in silently, came Ben Barth, Hiding Kneel, Morris Grant, Bruce and Pella. Jammed into Hugh Merrow's cluttered, solitary space they seemed an invasion, an explosion of bodies, though the studio was no smaller than the cleared-out schoolroom they'd been in a few minutes before.

The fading daylight shone too harshly on this scene. Pella closed the door behind her, and it seemed a small act of mercy.

"Here you go, Merrow, here's your beautiful Archbuilder," said Efram, thrusting Truth Renowned into the middle of the room. The Archbuilder stumbled, righted itself, a distant look in its eyes.

"What's that supposed to prove?" said Hugh Merrow in a soft voice. He didn't lift his head from its crutch of hands. "Truth is my model. Bringing—it—back here to me doesn't mean anything."

"You didn't say *it* last night."

"What's this all about?" said Clement.

"Linguistic dissension—" began Hiding Kneel from behind Clement.

"Wait, Kneel," said Clement, waving his hand. "I'm asking Efram."

"We were at Wa's, last night," said Efram. "Me, and Ben, and Merrow here. Having a drink. Wa's little general store turns into a place for drinking, after hours." He spread his hands to indicate the counter in Wa's shop. "I don't know if he'd let you family men in on it. Can't imagine you'd bother with it if he did. It's for us lonely types. But after Merrow got in his cups last night he started talking like he wasn't really all that lonely."

"That's ridiculous," Merrow burst out, looking up angrily at Efram.

"Going on about how beautiful *she* was, tearing his hair about it—"

"I was talking about my painting, the difficulty of capturing in a portrait—"

"You were talking about a hell of a lot more than that and you know it. And so does the native beauty here."

The accused Archbuilder stood helplessly between them, fronds depressed against its head.

"He was baiting me," said Hugh Merrow, turning to Clement. "He was feeding me drinks, first of all, and planting this idea, this thing he wanted to think—"

"Baiting and planting, now *de*bating," said Hiding Kneel.

"Yeah, and next comes mass debating," whispered Morris Grant to Bruce and Pella. Bruce shoved him, so hard that he stumbled forward and jarred a palette-table. Several thin tubes of paint fell and scattered on the floor.

"*Morris,*" said Joe Kincaid.

"It was Bruce!" Morris said plaintively.

Joe Kincaid put a hand heavily on the shoulder of each boy.

"Let's get the kids out of here," said Ben Barth. "Seems like keeping them away from all this is the whole point."

"I'm not convinced there is a point," said Clement evenly. "Apart from spreading innuendo."

"Well, they don't have to sit through this, whatever it is," said Joe Kincaid, guiding the boys to the door. "Bruce, Morris, Pella, why don't you—"

"Pella can stay," said Clement.

"Okay," said Joe, a little awkwardly. "You boys clear out, Pella can do what she wants—"

"I'd *prefer* it if she stayed," said Clement. "If that's all right with you, Pella."

Pella shrugged.

Efram watched, a hand on one hip, his mouth set into something like a grin, his eyebrows raised. The very image of smoldering patience. "Let her stay," he said. "Maybe she can help us sort this out."

Hugh Merrow let his head sink back into his hands.

Then Bruce and Morris were gone, and the room was all men and Archbuilders, the men tense, crushed, proud, the Archbuilders impossible to fathom. Men and Archbuilders and Pella. Only Doug Grant was near her age, and he burned with an aggrieved hostility that made him distant, unreachable. More alien than the Archbuilders.

Pella knew she stood as a marker of Clement's resistance to Efram. As with the pills, she'd become their battleground. She knew too that she counted as older because her mother was dead.

She fought not to think of what she'd seen at Merrow's studio. A deer saw it, she decided. Not me.

"Let's get to the bottom of this thing," said Efram. He pointed lackadaisically at Hugh Merrow. "I'd like you to tell the rest of these people what you told me at Wa's."

"I didn't tell you anything," said Merrow, his breath ragged.

"This isn't a tribunal," said Clement.

"I didn't say it was," said Efram. "I just want to ask the man some questions."

"Perhaps a reenactment—" suggested Hiding Kneel.

"Shut up, Kneel," said Ben Barth.

"Maybe it's time for your Archbuilder to talk," said Efram, pointing his thumb at Truth Renowned, "since you already did. Just give it permission, Merrow— it'll do what you tell it. Just like when you two are alone."

"I don't know what you're talking about," said Hugh Merrow, finding his courage so suddenly he seemed startled by it. "The conversation you're referring to didn't happen. Nothing happened." He turned to Clement, an appeal in his eyes. "I *paint* Archbuilders, Mr. Marsh. Along with a lot of other things. And last night I had a drink with Efram Nugent. He was drunk, I was drunk, we *talked* about a lot of things."

Merrow leaned back in his chair now, eyes hollow, and stroked his yellow beard absently. He didn't look at Truth Renowned. "*Efram* talked about some things that were on his mind," he went on. "Things that maybe excited his imagination, I don't know. I humored him. I allowed him to make certain insinuations. I laughed along. That was a mistake, I see now. But I haven't done anything wrong."

Truth Renowned just stood, arms braided, looking at the floor.

"There's at least one of us here who knows you're lying," said Efram. "Besides me, that is."

149

He turned, met Pella's eyes, seemed to look through them. She froze.

"How long do you think before your Archbuilder blurts something out, Merrow?" said Efram, still looking at Pella. "Or worse, does like Kneel here says and provides somebody with a reenactment?"

Pella breathed again. Efram meant it was the Archbuilder who knew. Though he'd said *at least.*

"You don't have any evidence," said Clement. He moved closer to Truth Renowned, perhaps hoping the alien would speak, defend itself. But no. And Hugh Merrow was less than useless again, huddled in his chair. "It's not enough to bully an Archbuilder into some confession," Clement went on. "You need proof of harm."

"What's that supposed to mean?" said Efram.

"Show not just that something happened, but that anyone was hurt by it if it did happen. That anyone cares, Efram."

"You don't grasp what's at stake here, Marsh. How do you know your proof won't come when an Archbuilder leads a kid off into the hills for some more of what Hugh Merrow's been teaching them? That's the kind of reenactment I'm talking about."

"That's a bit far-fetched—"

"You assume they make the same distinction between kids and adults that we do. Well, think again. Talk to the Archbuilders and you'll find they consider *themselves* children."

Clement said nothing.

Pella wanted Efram to be wrong, wanted that slow

malevolent voice to stumble and fall instead of endlessly rolling forward. But hadn't Hiding Kneel said the same thing in Clement's classroom—when?

The class was a distant memory now.

"Watch them with your kids," said Efram. "You'll see. They respond to children more than to you or me. Children and portrait painters."

"I respond excellently to you, Efram Nugent," said Hiding Kneel eagerly. "But then I had not gathered that you were not a child—"

"Don't clutter this up with your claptrap, Kneel," said Ben Barth.

"Yeah, quiet," said Doug Grant gratuitously.

"Regarding another Archbuilder, my claptrap might be deemed vital," said Hiding Kneel. "A necessary prerequisite to your own claptrap."

"Be vital if you got Truth Renowned talking," said Efram. "Otherwise—"

There Efram broke off. Pella thought he'd left his sentence unfinished. Then she heard the unintelligible bubbling noise that followed his words. She came slowly to the realization that he was speaking another language.

The string of sounds issuing from Efram's mouth was broken into the same laconic measures as his English. It was like nothing Pella had ever heard and at the same time seemed the absolute distillation of Efram, as if his persona had been converted out of language into pure and utterly revealing music, a song of lazy menace.

That much was revealed. But the meaning was hidden.

* * *

"What was that?" said Clement warily.

"Hey," said Joe Kincaid. "You speak pretty good Archbuilder."

"I thought nobody—" started Clement.

He stopped because Truth Renowned was bubbling back at Efram, offering its own quavering, high-pitched version of the same noises.

"Not *Archbuilder,*" said Ben Barth quietly, chidingly, to Clement and Joe. "They call that stuff *Table Talk.*"

Truth Renowned paused, fronds rustling, then bubbled on, unstoppable now. The word *Merrow* jumped out, obvious like an off-note in a familiar melody.

Hugh Merrow stared at Truth Renowned, plainly as baffled as Clement.

"Efram just told Kneel to shut the hell up," whispered Ben Barth. "To let Truth do the talking."

At last the Archbuilder fell silent. Efram nodded, apparently satisfied.

Doug Grant said, "What, Efram? You find anything out?" His eyes darted wildly from Efram to Clement to the Archbuilders.

"Tell us, Efram," said Clement. "What did Truth Renowned say to you?"

"This meeting is over," said Efram, turning away.

"That's what it said?" said Clement. "That the meeting is over?"

"That's what *I* said," said Efram. "I'm calling it done."

It was ludicrous. Had a meeting even begun?

With Efram, talk was all interruptions. He was like the Archbuilder landscape, a series of things broken off.

Pella herself felt broken off.

"I've learned all I need to," said Efram. "Unless somebody else wants to add something." He looked at Pella and she felt the blood steam in her cheeks.

She hated him.

"I'll let you worry about your own kids from here on," he said. "Someone's lying, but let the lie stand."

"You didn't get what you were after," said Clement. "You're afraid you're wrong. Admit it."

"The one who can back me up isn't talking," said Efram. "Let's leave it at that."

He didn't stare at her this time, but he didn't have to. She was like a wound, stinging freshly in the open air.

"In the meantime," he went on, "Truth Renowned isn't going to hang around Merrow anymore. To get its portrait painted, or anything else." Efram's hand rose, to draw invisible pictures of all his words left unsaid. "That's its own decision, and it's good enough for me. Whatever happened, it's stopping here."

"We'll make sure of it, too," said Doug Grant, glaring at the Archbuilder.

Merrow slumped down in his chair again, hair in his twisted fingers, back bent like it bore a world.

"Is that what you said?" Clement asked Truth Renowned. "Why not tell the rest of us? There's nothing to be afraid of."

Truth Renowned didn't speak.

"The question relevant to me is whether Hugh Merrow might relinquish the incomplete portrait," said Hiding Kneel. "In that eventuality I might complete the work—"

Merrow got out of his chair and moved in a frenzy to the painting turned against the wall. He thrust the stretched canvas roughly at Hiding Kneel. "Take it, and get out. Get out of my house, all of you!"

Hiding Kneel accepted the painting gracefully and bowed its head, tendrils tumbling forward.

And then Kneel and Truth Renowned swayed smoothly and wordlessly to the door. As though all along they'd only awaited Merrow's command, as though for them this was a meeting *Merrow* had called. But as Hugh Merrow stood, empty-handed now, his shrill outburst ringing in their ears, his moment of authority leaked away. Back to Efram. Merrow sank into his chair.

Pella willed herself to meet Efram's eyes, and saw only distance. He was done with his shadow play. His disaster. Efram didn't really care about Hugh Merrow, Pella understood.

What, then? Could this have been for her sake?

The door open, the room flooded with sun. Pella walked out onto Merrow's porch. Joe Kincaid, Ben Barth, and Doug Grant abandoned the squalid house, began back up the ridge.

"It's good you came," said Efram to Clement. "It

should have been you in the first place. I'm no politician."

"This wasn't a politician's job—" Clement stopped, crossed up. Efram had made him complicit again.

Hugh Merrow didn't look up. Efram glanced at him, then raised an eyebrow at Clement. "Let's clear out. Leave Merrow alone with his thoughts. And his *pictures.*"

Clement didn't move.

"If you want to talk more," said Efram, "keep Wa's place in mind. After hours, I mean."

Pella thought, he's inviting him to *school*.

Twelve

A household deer was running across the valley. It had no destination. It darted from shadow to shadow, uninterested in the towers or arches that cast them.

Its pure interest was in being a thing running, and its concern in knowing where the human places lay in the landscape was only to avoid those places, the identical homesteads.

So it ran.

From the left, another deer dashed up alongside the first. They ran zigzagging, bound together, though it wasn't love that bound them. There wasn't anything nearly that strong between the deer. Nor was it fondness, or concern. Only adjacency.

It was a relationship that could be sustained, didn't conceal any pitfalls. It *worked*, adjacency. Like running worked. So they zipped along in flawless formation, jumping a gap in the valley floor, one, two. They ignored the sky, which had nothing to do with them.

They weren't afraid. It was running time, not hiding time.

Maybe today wouldn't be a spying day at all, thought the first of the deer. Maybe for once they didn't care what the humans or Archbuilders were doing.

Then the second of the household deer skipped off to the right, ducked off a ledge and over, into a gully. There was a puff of dust in the air where it had last stood. After that, nothing. The first deer stopped, ran alone for a minute, then, recognizing the spot, turned and slipped into the gully from around the corner of a broken edifice.

The second deer wasn't visible, but the first knew where it was.

This would be a spying day after all.

The toppled spire that the girl had made into her hideaway had been a convenient hovel for the deer, before the girl had arrived. They didn't object to her occupying it, however. The deer didn't object to things. Only kept an eye on them. Anyway, the girl's presence didn't keep the deer from going there. It simply changed it from a place where they hid and nibbled at the potatoes that grew in the corner to a place where they hid and watched the girl.

The doorway was half-buried in rubble. The girl had been at work again, disguising it. And there was something new, set just inside the entrance. A bundle, two bottles of pills inside a knotted plastic bag, labelled in block letters, FOR PELLA, and signed with the single letter B.

So the sneaky boy had been around. The household deer knew him, knew about his visits here.

The first deer climbed over the obstacles and slipped inside. The second deer had settled in the corner near the sealed bottles of water, with another deer who had already been inside, watching. The girl was curled in her usual position, in a sickly looking sleep, clutching the blanket, which was bunched under her arms.

The first deer felt a queasy sort of contempt for the girl. The feeling was betraying. The deer knew it shouldn't care, knew it was thinking and feeling too much, knew it should only be a set of feet and eyes. Taking a post behind the water bottles and between the other two deer, it pretended it too was watching indifferently, just keeping track. But in truth it felt an inarticulate misery. Looking at the girl as she lay there was somehow overwhelming, nauseating.

The problem was the girl was a mixed-up thing, a combination of two things. If not more. She was growing a new body, a woman's body, raw new shapes under her clothes. It made the deer tired and annoyed to see it. If only the blanket were covering the girl the deer wouldn't have to consider the deformed body, the new breasts.

The girl's body was *pretentious* with womanhood.

The girl shifted, and suddenly the deer was nervous, not wanting to see her waken. That had to be avoided. It was a mistake to come here and look. When the girl stirred further, tossing her impossible, objectionable new body, tugging uselessly at the blanket, the deer jumped out of its place with the others and scrabbled out of the chamber and across the rubble at the entrance, as much in a panic as if threatened by a poking stick or foot.

The other two deer caught up with the first a moment later, and they climbed together up the steepest side of the ravine, back onto the flat of the valley.

The deer ran to deny its mistake now, to forget the person in the chamber. Running to forget wasn't as pure as running for no reason at all, but it was still a consolation to zip along implacably, three now, making silent ribbons across the surface of the world. So when the others halted the first halted too. Wishing to stay buried deep in deer life, in skittish curiosity, it noticed too late that they'd stopped to peek over a crest at an unexpected sight. A figure huddled at the base of a ruin, in a nest of vines, fiddling with an array of objects.

The place was a nowhere on the human map of the valley, as distant from any house or trail as the girl's hideaway. There shouldn't have been anyone there. But there was. The figure was bent, with its back to them, impossible to identify from this distance except as human, not Archbuilder. And young.

The other two deer, being deer, snuck up for a better view. The first had no reasonable choice except to follow.

It was the girl's brother. Raymond Marsh. He squatted in the center of a half ring of trinkets and photographs, fetishes placed carefully in the vines and rubble, in the shade of a jagged ruin.

All three of the deer crept insistently nearer, the first compelled by something more than companionship with the others now. Was Raymond assembling his own hideaway, a place to sleep during the day? But that wasn't it, not exactly. The deer craned its neck to see. The photographs were of Caitlin, pictures taken in Brooklyn. Some were cameos, Caitlin-faces trimmed out of group photos, family scenes. The rest was jewelry and keepsakes, souvenirs of Caitlin, borrowed or stolen from Clement's drawer.

Raymond was mourning his mother.

At this the deer confessed to herself what she'd been evading. That she was Pella. Visiting herself in the hideout hadn't stirred her out of her disguise from herself, but Raymond had.

It was a small, vivid loss, like waking from a dream of solving a problem to find that the solution didn't make sense, that the problem had only been contemplated, not solved.

Raymond went on touching the photographs, adjusting their places, his head bowed. Lost in his own conjured space. Had he come here before? Pella wondered. Was this a regular spot, were the objects stored in some cubby or pit in the rocks? Or did the ritual consist of walking out into the valley and arranging a new shrine each time?

Maybe there was no ritual. This could be the first

time. But she feared she'd discovered too late. She'd been ignoring Raymond, and now it turned out he was mortifying himself in sorrow.

Pella was not the only one trying to find her mother somewhere in the valley.

She wanted to reach out, touch his shoulder. Instead she ran into the middle of his circle, in front of his folded knees, and stared up at him stupid, voiceless, wide-eyed. Raymond looked up, and swept his hand, whisking her out of the ring. Then he turned and saw the other two deer staring from behind him. Before he could reach them they'd darted off to a safer distance. He waved his arm anyway, trying to frighten them away.

Pella trembled in confusion behind a fragment of pillar, but Raymond was already back to his fugue. Household deer were a familiar interruption anywhere. Not worth a second glance.

Still a deer, Pella rushed back to the house, looking for Clement. The house was empty, but there were noises in back, from Clement's new garden. She went to look.

It was David, and Martha Kincaid, and Morris Grant. They knelt in the planted rows, Morris rooting in the dirt with a stick on either side of a row of tiny sprouts.

"See how they're so small?" Morris was saying. "That's because the deer eat the roots."

"How?" said David.

"From underneath, they dig tunnels. They have tunnels all over the place, you know."

"I thought they were small because they're baby plants," said Martha, squinting in the bright sun, knitting her forehead.

"No, they're dying. See, that's why Efram keeps all his stuff in pots, because of the deer tunnels." He twisted his stick in the ground, closer and closer to the new sprouts.

Pella thought, Deer tunnels?

Morris was playing expert, like Bruce Kincaid. The difference being Morris was making it up as he went along. Pella wondered what idiocies she would hear, if she followed this little group through a day.

Morris worked his forked stick under a sprout, right below the soil line, then jerked it up out of the ground, tearing it. "See?" he said. "No roots."

"Clement just planted that," said David. His protest was uncertain, at best.

"Well it isn't going to grow," said Morris admonishingly, and holding it on the extended stick like it was tainted, he flicked it away, to wither on a bare rock.

Pella wished she *could* tunnel under Morris, hollow out all but a crust of earth, so that he fell through and was humiliated, went home muddy and sniffling. She wished Bruce were here to give him a shove.

"Hugh Merrow's going to move away," said Morris.

"He is?" said David. "Why?"

"How do you know?" said Martha.

"Because everybody hates him. Doug told me about it."

"Everybody hates him why?" said David.

"He fooled around with Archbuilders."

Pella went back on her silent feet to the porch. The urge to hear more was checked by her disinclination to play the part of the deer in Morris's malicious fantasies, to be screamed at and chased with a stick.

She wished Clement were here, wished she could take his hand and direct him to Raymond, out in the valley, direct him to the torn sprout on the rock, and say, *Caitlin's not here anymore. Look what's happening to your family. To your lettuce and chard.*

She searched the house again, looking for Clement or for clues to where he'd gone. But the house was empty. No, that was wrong. It was the valley that was simply empty. The house was something worse. It was a failure, a travesty. The signs were everywhere. Here was her room, where she did nothing but sleep, and that only in short, angry bursts. Here Raymond's toys, abandoned for pictures of Caitlin. Here Clement's dust-gathering computer—who was there for Clement to conference with? Caitlin had said Clement was here to do Clement things, but there weren't any Clement things to do. Clement was nobody now. Here in a corner of the living room was the stack of chairs, forgotten since the school disaster. Here was the jar that held David's potato fish until the morning, a week ago, when they'd suddenly died. Here on the table, a batch of plastic-wrapped sandwiches with a note, reading, *Juice in fridge. Dinner at Kincaids' tonight, meet you there. Clement.*

And only a household deer to witness this. But not for long. She dashed across the porch, into the unhaunted, impersonal emptiness of the ruined land. As she ran she felt and heard herself jerking with little shrill hiccups. The deer was doing what the girl in her own body hadn't done since that day, which seemed ages ago now, when she'd climbed into her father's lap: crying.

Diana Eastling was back. Pella in her deer body had scampered up the side of a column and unexpectedly seen the signs of life from Diana's house. Lit windows, a pile of burned garbage in the backyard that still smoldered. Pella checked herself. It could be Efram. But if Diana Eastling were there—

Finding Diana Eastling was better than finding Clement. Pella would make her listen, tell her everything, Pella's whole strange new life. Diana Eastling knew about the people here, no matter how much she tried to play dumb. She'd explain what Efram wanted, and Pella would use that knowledge to protect Clement. And Diana Eastling knew about the planet, too. She'd help Pella decide whether to take the pills Bruce had stolen for her.

Diana Eastling was who she'd been looking for, she decided. She half-ran, half-tumbled down the column and started over the ridge. She'd only make sure Diana was there, then dash back to the hiding place and reclaim her human body. Then come back and knock on the door—

She stopped short. On the porch was Clement's bicycle.

Enthusiasm suspended, she made her way inside, through an open back window.

Clement and Diana Eastling sat together on the couch in the living room, and even if Diana Eastling hadn't had her left leg across Clement's right leg, Pella would have understood instantly from the dreamy, self-congratulatory smiles they both wore. But anyway, there *was* her leg, over his. Pella snuck up under the kitchen table and stared, and the crossed legs, the point where Clement's and Diana's bodies intersected, seemed to burn itself into her vision. It was so simple, one limb piled on another, two dumb slabs of meat, yet it was like an optical illusion too, some impossible four-dimensional figure whose existence warped the rest of the world out of shape.

"That's part of why I left," Diana Eastling was saying. "I didn't know what to do, it was ridiculous."

"I wondered," said Clement.

"You were being such a dolt," she continued. "I couldn't stand watching you fumbling around, getting your sea legs here. It was going to keep me from liking you. And I was beginning to like you."

"That's unfair."

Pella was holding her breath, trying not to make a sound. But she couldn't have made a sound if she'd wanted to, not in this body.

"I think it was very fair," said Diana Eastling. "You were full of stupid questions, bad guesses. You hadn't even met Efram yet. I wasn't going to walk you through that. I'm not fond of that sort of thing."

"You wanted me to meet Efram first? Why was that important?"

"He was worked up about your coming. The two of you were obviously headed toward some tedious male thing. And God, if you haven't worked it out yet, please don't tell me about it."

"So I seem different now."

"You learned to lead with something other than your stupid questions, with me, anyway. That's different enough."

"Just because I'm not leading with my questions doesn't mean I've gotten answers for them," said Clement carefully.

"I shouldn't have mentioned Efram. Now you sound like you think you're talking to him."

"Efram's tedious male thing is hounding Hugh Merrow out of this town, Diana."

"I credit both of you with the tedious male thing. Not just Efram. That's the first thing." She swung her leg away, then abruptly rose from the couch and went to the table. As she loomed up Pella shrank back into the tumbleweeds of dust along the floor, and the upper half of Diana Eastling's body disappeared above the table's edge. Clement remained on the couch, in the same position. Pella watched him through Diana Eastling's knees.

Then Diana Eastling turned and walked back to him, lighting a cigarette while she spoke. "The second is that what's happened, what's happening, between us here—it has nothing to do with Efram, or Hugh Merrow, or anything else outside this room. It isn't an alliance."

"What is it?"

"A *liaison*." She blew out smoke. Pella couldn't see her face.

Clement smiled.

A blackened match-head bounced to the floor under the table, still issuing a thread of smoke.

"Hugh Merrow made things difficult for himself around here from the moment he arrived," said Diana Eastling wearily. "That's not Efram's fault. But I'm getting drawn into justifying Efram's behavior, and I don't want to do that. Maybe whatever's being done to Hugh Merrow is blatantly unfair, Clement. But don't bring it into this."

"That's clear enough."

"Is it? Good." She paused. "I came here to make my own space, Clement. Most of us did."

"I'm learning."

"Yes, you are."

Diana Eastling still had the edge in her voice that Pella had admired, but it was too late for it to mean anything anymore. Her leg across Clement's had ruined everything.

Diana Eastling reached out, cigarette between her fingers, and touched Clement's hair.

Set him on fire, Pella thought.

"Kiss me now," said Diana Eastling. "You're letting me talk too much. I don't like that any better than your questions."

He got up from the couch and pulled her to him. She held the cigarette away as they kissed, then drew on it when they finished.

"Mmmm."

"What's going to happen?"

"Shhh."

Through her anger at them both, Pella felt pity for Clement. He was alone, and being in Diana Eastling's arms only made it less noble, more pathetic. Didn't he hear her cynicism? Couldn't he see how little use she had for him? They didn't understand each other, had nothing in common. Pella was certain she knew them both better than they knew each other, Clement better than he knew himself. Clement on Diana Eastling's couch was like Raymond at his shrine. Pitiful.

Then Pella's anger overtook her pity. Clement and Diana had betrayed her. It was Pella who was most alone in the end, knowing all she knew. She was in charge of Clement's aloneness, but he'd abandoned Pella to hers.

Thirteen

Pella was off-balance from the start. She woke back into herself and left her warren, almost stumbling across the plastic bag of pills. She detached Bruce's note and let it flutter away. The wind died, then rose again, the note tipping corner over corner across the cracked gully, a square wheel, until it vanished in the glare. Then she took the bag and clambered up the grade, and that was when she saw Efram, at the top of the ridge, hand on his hip, eyes narrowed. He might have paused in midstep as he passed or been waiting there for hours, she couldn't know. After that she never caught her breath.

He fell into step beside her, one of his strides for two of hers.

"Pella Marsh," he said. His voice was far-away engines rumbling, the subway rushing underfoot. "What do you know."

She ignored the words, but walked with him, not veering away. For days she'd avoided his house, frightened to approach him even invisible, as a deer. Now her fear had been replaced by a furious compulsion to match his pace, to walk unafraid.

"I said *Pella Marsh,*" said Efram. "What do you know."

"What do I know?" said Pella. She thought of Clement and Diana Eastling. I know too much, she thought.

Efram laughed. "That's right, Pella Marsh. What do you know?"

"More than you," she said. "I'll say one thing, though—you say my name as much as an Archbuilder."

"Which Archbuilder?"

"I didn't mean a particular one."

She clutched the bag of pills, refusing to try and hide it. The plastic was transparent, plain what was inside. But Efram didn't comment on it. Without seeming to change his stride he increased his pace, and Pella fell behind. He didn't look back at her.

She hurried to catch up, not knowing why she did. He'd sought her out, hadn't he? Why didn't he speak? But maybe she was wrong, maybe he'd just happened to be there.

A household deer curled around the side of a craggy shelf in the rock and skittered into their path. Efram leaned down and in one huge, smooth motion swept the back of his hand across the tops of his shoes. He'd calculated the deer's path perfectly. His knuckles collided with the frail body at the lowest point in the arc of his swing, and the deer flew up over the top of the rocks.

The deer skidded in the dust, feet scrabbling as it

righted itself, then dashed away. The violence was so effortless that it had a kind of poetry, so fast that it seemed possible it hadn't happened at all. Efram held his hand in front of him, palm facing the ground, and glanced at his knuckles for just a moment, as if he were checking to see that nail polish had dried. His vast, lazy stride never faltered.

"This isn't your house!" said Pella.

"You're still here?" he said, turning to grin at her.

This absurdity made her feel again that she was the audience for something staged. But all she could say was "What are you afraid of, anyway?"

"From the deer?"

"Yeah."

"Let me put it this way, Pella Marsh." He pointed at her, his finger descending from the air. "When I see you up and on your feet the deer don't worry me all that much. But I still don't want them around."

He handled her secrets so casually, like they and she were features of the landscape now.

She *was* a feature of the landscape.

She and Efram had that in common, she because she ran over it, hid in it, and he because he was like a chunk of it, broken off and ambulatory. The last intact tower.

They belonged together, out here walking in the sun. She skipped to keep up with him. The bag of pills swung at her side, the bunched plastic sweaty in her grasp.

Her objection to his swipe at the deer suddenly seemed hopelessly naive, something Clement would say.

As if a human in a diving suit had tried to dictate that some ancient monumental whale not brush away a pilot fish, or gobble up the plankton in its path.

That was why she had to be her Pella-self with him, why she couldn't slip through doorways at his feet to spy on him. She had to be more than plankton to him, more than a buzzing gnat. She wanted his notice.

"Where are . . . you going?" said Pella. She'd almost said *we*.

"My house," said Efram. "You coming?"

"Is Doug Grant there?"

"You want to see Doug Grant?"

"Nope."

"Well he's not there. He doesn't live at my place, he lives with his parents. Nobody's there."

"Where's Ben Barth?"

"You taking a census? Ben Barth's out, he's helping Hugh Merrow."

"Helping him with what?"

"How should I know? Something he needed help with."

"I thought you didn't like Hugh Merrow."

"What's that got to do with it?" His exasperation made her childishly pleased. "Ben helps everybody with everything. He doesn't have to like them. And I don't tell him what to do. You coming?"

"Sure."

The reason went unspoken, like it was obvious. But in fact the only reasons she could conceive were ridiculous, so thrilling and objectionable that she had to think instead that they were walking together to his house for no reason at all.

They finished the trek in silence. The household deer kept away. Indeed, the closer they got to his house the fewer Pella saw. She wondered if over time the deer had learned to avoid his place.

As they came into Efram's potted garden, the sprawl of wire-mesh-covered planters, scattered tools and refuse that surrounded his house, Pella felt that they were crossing into an enchanted circle, a zone of meaning. His house wasn't like the others. It was older, finer. She'd arrived on the Planet of the Archbuilders at last. The rest had been a facade. But she barely had time to measure her response, to place herself, before they stepped inside. And inside, it was another world.

Efram's main room was a reconstruction of an Archbuilder interior, like the fallen fragment that Pella used as her hideaway, but larger. Efram-sized. The surface was scraped clean, shattered shelves and ornaments painstakingly glued together, whorls of stone and knobs of translucent glass restored, polished until they gleamed. Lit by tiny colored bulbs hidden everywhere in the crevices, the room glinted like a jewel box as she stepped inside. Hung on the walls and piled on the shelves were Archbuilder medicine bottles, tools, appliances, other objects she couldn't identify, some corroded, fragmented like the towers, others glistening. The reconstruction made up the four walls of the room, blocking the windows, narrowing the space by half. As Efram closed the door behind her, squeezing away the last margin of sunlight, the effect was that of stepping from the day into the inner chamber of a star-lost spaceship, or an ancient tomb.

He waved his hand at a small couch tucked inside the convex Archbuilder wall, and she went to it, stumbling a little. She sat, dropping the bag of pills to the left of the couch. Efram still hadn't taken notice of them.

"I thought you didn't like Archbuilders," she said.

"You said the same thing about me and Hugh Merrow," he said, raising his eyebrows. "You're awfully concerned with what I don't like."

"Well, isn't it true?"

"The Archbuilders I don't like aren't the ones that built these walls," he said. "They're the ones that didn't bother to keep the walls from falling apart. You want something to drink?"

She nodded.

He pushed open a door to what looked, from her vantage on the couch, like a normal kitchen, illuminated by a sunlit window. It was then, in the light from the kitchen, that she saw the rifle mounted on a ledge inside the Archbuilder wall. It was one thing that had nothing to do with Archbuilders, she knew.

In a moment he returned with glasses for both of them, and closed the kitchen door. Pella sipped her drink. It was some kind of soda. Root beer, but pale, almost clear.

She swallowed a mouthful and said, "I have a place

like this." She surprised herself with the words, the boastful way they sounded.

He stood over her, watching. All he said was, "Good."

"Sit down," she said. "You're too tall." She felt afraid, but again her words came out manic, assertive. Her cheeks were glowing with heat. She imagined they shone like beacons in this room, that they glowed like the colored lights. She wanted to dip her fingers in the soda and wet her cheeks with it, feel the cool bubbles on the heat of her skin. But Efram was staring at her.

He laughed again and sat on the couch beside her. He took a long drink from his glass, closing his eyes while he tipped his head back and swallowed, another little performance for her to watch. The color of his soda was different from hers. It looked darker, like whiskey. She wanted to be drinking what he was drinking, and to close her eyes while she swallowed.

He put his glass on the floor between his feet. "Why'd you come here, Pella Marsh?"

"Stop using my whole name."

It was actually the least of her objections. She hoped he'd withdraw the dangerous, unnecessary question.

"Why'd you come here . . . *Pella.*"

"To your house?"

He shook his head, and waved his hand like the suggestion was exasperating. "Planet of the Archbuilders."

"Family, stupid." She thought of Clement sitting with Diana Eastling, her leg over his. Family.

"You're old enough to make your own decisions."

She nearly corrected him, then decided she liked the sound of it. She put her glass to her lips to have something to do with her mouth other than speak. She drank, then held the side of the glass to her burning cheek.

"I guess you do what Clement tells you," said Efram, half-contemptuously, half as though he'd realized her connection to Clement for the first time.

I'm here because of Caitlin, Pella thought. But she didn't want to tell him that, either. She didn't want to talk to him about her parents. It made her too much the pilot fish beside the whale.

She felt drowsy and crazed at once. Efram was drinking the whiskey—if that's what he was drinking—but she was the one getting drunk. Drunk on the Archbuilder walls, drunk on Efram's big, disastrous body so close to her. Drunk on the way he moved his arms.

She lifted her leg, entranced, and draped it over Efram's knee.

He didn't push it away. She couldn't bring herself to look to see his expression. She closed her eyes and leaned her head back against the couch, and said, "Explain to me about the Archbuilders."

It seemed like a thousand years before he spoke.

"Which Archbuilders?" His voice was neutral. Her leg felt like a twig across his giant thigh. It twitched, pulsed. She felt sure he could feel the blood beat in it the way she could. Like her whole leg was a single vein.

"The ones you hate," she said, eyes still shut.

It was a while again before he said anything. His leg was perfectly still, and it—or more precisely, the place where her leg met his—was the only thing in her universe, until his voice floated down to join it. "Hiding Kneel and Truth Renowned, those types aren't what I call Archbuilders," he said. "They're what the Archbuilders left behind."

His words came to her like she was underwater. But she understood. "You mean the ones that went into space."

"That's right. They were something a little different than the sorry batch we've got lurking around here. They remade their planet, built a civilization, and then they figured out a way to do the greatest thing anyone's ever done—explore the stars. The rabble around here are just the lazy, stupid ones that didn't want to go."

Pella tried to imagine this exodus, the great world that had been here, then flown away. Somehow she couldn't picture the arches any way other than destroyed, couldn't imagine the Archbuilders any different from how they were now. What she pictured instead were *people* living here, building starships. People like Efram, exactly. Maybe that's what he pictured too.

She said, dreamily, "Someone had to stay."

"Could be that's what they told themselves at the start of it, Pella."

Pella, her eyes closed, head back on the couch, felt that she and his tremendous leg and the couch were in one place together, while his voice was piped down from some impossibly distant other place. Perhaps from space, from aboard an Archbuilder starship.

"But look what it's done to them," he went on. "They passed up the chance to find new frontiers, became a bunch of good-for-nothing navel-gazers instead. They made this planet into a hell of luxury—the weather control, the free food. And it made them into hothouse creatures picking through their own memories of greatness. They're not a civilization anymore."

Was Efram really using words like *navel-gazers* and *hothouse?* He sounded like an Archbuilder. Like Hiding Kneel. Or was she beginning to fall asleep and dream elaborations on his talk? Was he really talking at all?

"The Archbuilders who left built this place as a challenge to us, Pella. Why else do you think we can breathe the air, drink the water? They invited us up to get a look around here, give us a taste of getting off Earth, to face us with a choice. We could try to follow them to the stars, to the real frontier, or we could bog down here with these idiots, get lulled by the weather and the free food and the atmosphere of complacent degenerate buffoonery."

It felt as though her leg and his were floating upward, that the immense weight of them together had been released and that they were now moving toward the ceiling. The words—some of them had to be his, she could never have invented *complacent degenerate buffoonery,* didn't feel at all responsible for *bog* or *lulled*—swam in her consciousness.

"Calling them idiots is too generous. They're sexual deviants, most of them. That didn't matter when it was just me and Ben and a couple of others living up here, but if they touch the children I'll kill them."

She was falling into a nerve-racked sleep. It came

over her irresistibly, like a fever. For a moment she thought she might escape into some nearby household deer, and by doing so find clarity, open her eyes. She could sneak around to Efram's house, find her way inside and watch this encounter from a neutral corner, sort out the confusion of bodies and words.

But this wasn't that sort of sleep, and besides, there wasn't a household deer nearby. She was only slipping deeper into herself. Nobody would see what happened in this room unless she opened her eyes, and opening her eyes was impossible.

"I kill them already, actually. I roast them in my kiln in the backyard and eat them. My little joke— Archbuilders eat potatoes, I eat Archbuilders. They both grow wild around here."

She was dreaming, and in her dream she protested, illogically, Can't he see that I'm asleep? Why won't he stop talking? Doesn't he know that I'll believe whatever he says?

"If your dad doesn't leave, I'll kill him too. This isn't the place for him to practice his politics. He should go home. Maybe he'll leave you here, though. I wouldn't mind that."

Efram nudged her awake, speaking her name. His voice was gentle now.

She looked up at him foggily.

"We'd better get you home," he said.

Her leg had slipped, or been lifted, from his. Their

bodies hadn't touched anywhere but that one place. That one place burned. She didn't speak, just rubbed her eyes.

She had slept, she was sure now. The words, at least some of them, had been a dream.

She would never know which ones.

Efram got up from the couch and opened the door. The sky was dark now. The colored lights in the room leaked out weakly into the night. Even the edge of the porch was barely visible.

"I'll walk you back. Come on."

"My—we're having dinner at the Kincaids'."

"Then I'll walk you to the Kincaids'."

They left his compound and set off along the dim paths, Efram ahead, his step sure. Pella's boldness was gone, but so was her fear. Those extremes had been rolled together, blunted by her strange, deep sleep.

Efram walked too fast for her, but she didn't complain, didn't speak at all, just broke into short skipping runs to catch up the whole way back. He glanced down at her half-indifferently, like she was a parcel to be delivered now. Their afternoon together was over.

The Kincaids' house was lit, and Pella could see activity bubbling behind the curtains. Efram stopped outside the penumbra of spilling light, at a rocky bend in the path, and lifted his heavy finger to point at the house. "There you go."

She went ahead of him to the house, and didn't turn until she reached the porch. He stood like a monolith in the shadows, watching. She thought she saw him nod at her. She went inside.

Fourteen

The girl walked into the lit room blinking. It was cluttered with life, a chaos of activity, demands. The two families were around the table, her father, her brothers, the Kincaids. Bruce Kincaid, watching her. The meal was nearly over, empty plates smeared—except her father's. He was helping himself to green potatoes from a huge bowl. Joe Kincaid was pouring him a drink. He'd just come in, she saw. Like her, he'd been out in the valley, living his secret life. Out in the valley, now sealed in darkness. The girl moved to the table still in a kind of trance.

"Your father was worried," said Ellen Kincaid, taking Pella by the elbow and hurrying her to a seat at a clean table setting.

"Here you go," said Joe, loading up her plate.

"Are you sick?" said David. "You look sick."

"I fell asleep," she said. She started to push the plate of steaming mash away, then realized she was hungry. She took her fork and directed a chunk of the lukewarm flavorless stew into her mouth, chewing intently so she wouldn't be expected to speak. She didn't want to look at anyone, didn't want to answer questions. She knew where they'd all been. Wasn't that enough?

"Well, eat up," said Joe Kincaid jauntily. "You'll keep us waiting for dessert."

In reply, Pella only chewed. Clement had as much on his plate as she did. If she was keeping them from dessert, so was he. He'd barely started. She must have come near to running into him, on the paths back out of the valley.

Back from their *liaisons*.

"Can we be excused?" said Martha Kincaid.

"Sure," said Joe Kincaid. Martha and David ran from the table, almost stumbling over each other, and disappeared into the back of the house. Raymond got up too, but somberly, and flopped into a chair.

Bruce moved from his place, but only to sit closer to Pella. "You get the package?" he whispered.

Pella nodded. Then, confused, she looked down at the floor beside her chair. Where was the bag of pills?

On the floor beside Efram's couch, in his Archbuilder cave of a living room.

Bruce said, "What's the matter?"

"Nothing."

"But you got them?"

"Yes. Shhh." She tried to calculate the meaning of

her mistake, the trajectory of a fall in progress. What would Efram do with the pills? Get Bruce in trouble for stealing them? That was the least of it. Efram would think of something worse, something she couldn't guess at.

Unless—shouldn't Efram want her to take the pills? In that he was on her side, wasn't he?

"You'll take them, right?" said Bruce.

"Quiet," she said. "Don't talk about it here."

But nobody was listening. Clement babbled blithely to Joe and Ellen Kincaid about Diana Eastling's field trip, her study of Archbuilder science. Pella wondered if Joe and Ellen knew about Clement and Diana's affair. Probably. Probably they knew and imagined they were helping *keep it from the children.*

She wanted to get away from the table, out of the house. She picked up her plate. "Come on," she said to Bruce. "Let's sit on the porch."

"You were asleep when I came by," said Bruce. "You slept all day?"

"I guess." It was an odd lie, given that she was on the verge of nodding off here, on the edge of the porch, her plate in her lap.

The lights of the house were behind her. She knew Bruce couldn't read her face. She looked up at the shadowy ridge where Efram had last stood. She could imagine him still there, a little back, veiled in darkness, watching the house.

In her imagination he always stood there, in a place just out of sight, watching.

"Aren't you scared?" said Bruce.

"No," she lied. Whatever he meant she should be scared of.

They sat not speaking for a moment, then she asked, "Where'd you get the pills?"

"Wa's. The delivery guy from Southport came through. Doug Grant was hanging around, and some Archbuilders. I just stole them when everybody was out back, unpacking stuff."

"Why do you want to hang around with Doug Grant?"

"I don't know. I mean, I don't."

"He's a jerk," said Pella, surprising herself with the force of it. "He thinks he's Efram."

Bruce didn't respond. Probably he wanted to be Efram, too.

"While you're sucking up to Doug Grant, my brother and your sister are Morris Grant's little slaves," she said.

"I can't help it if they want to follow him everywhere. Tell Raymond to watch David."

"Raymond isn't bigger than Morris. You are."

But it was hopeless to expect Bruce to chaperone David and Martha and Morris. The unity of the larger group was an illusion. It had formed because Bruce was following Pella, and so were Pella's brothers, just as Martha was following her older brother. Then Morris had attached himself to the five of them. When Pella retired to her turret, her hole in the ground, the group dispersed, each member seeking new alliances.

Like her family, now that Caitlin was gone.

"Okay, okay," said Joe. "Here, we've got something unusual, they were selling it down at Wa's today. Somebody at Southport concocted a kind of ice cream, Archbuilder ice cream, made from ice potatoes. Bruce, why don't you help get some bowls?"

Joe dished out the imported dessert, and it was passed around the table.

"This isn't like ice cream," said Bruce.

"It's really *sweet,*" said Martha, making a face.

"I hate it," said David.

"I don't know, it's not bad," said Clement. "Sweet and gooey and cold—is this vanilla?"

"Remember when you made that pudding from tea potatoes and froze it?" said Bruce to his father. "*That* was more like ice cream."

"Yeah, but Bruce, that was from tea potatoes," said Martha.

"So?"

"So this is more like ice cream," explained Martha patiently. "Because it's made from ice potatoes. Because of the word ice."

"I think it's crappy," said Bruce. "Did Wa even taste this stuff? He bought about fifty pounds of it off the delivery guy."

"Bought *from,* not *off.*"

There was a knock on the door. Pella's throat tightened with fear. Thinking of him on the ridge, she'd somehow summoned him back.

What if he'd brought the bag of pills, to return to her, out in front of Clement? Could he want to be that disastrous?

But when Joe opened the door it wasn't Efram. On the porch stood Hugh Merrow. His clothes were rumpled and dusty, his expression desperate. He stared at the families gathered at the table, the children spooning up their dessert, as though facing a firing squad.

"I was looking for Clement," he said. "I hope I'm not interrupting."

"Of course not," said Joe. "Come in. Let us give you something—a drink."

"No. I can't stay. I just wanted to—I checked your house, I went inside and saw your note. So I knew you were here." His voice was miserable, like it was wrung from damp cloth.

"Right," said Clement. "Here I am."

"I wanted to thank you. Before I leave."

"Leave for where?"

"Away from here."

"You don't mean permanently."

Hugh Merrow just nodded.

"How—what about your stuff? Your paintings?"

"The man from Southport is back at my place, loading his truck. I paid him to change his schedule. We'll leave as soon as I'm packed. There's a ship back later this week."

"Back? To Earth, you mean?" asked Joe Kincaid. The rest of them were still and silent, hanging on the conversation, even David and Martha.

"Toronto," said Hugh Merrow.

"That's ridiculous," Clement burst out. "How can you want to go back? Why are you letting him do that to you?"

"I'm not letting anyone do anything. I've decided to leave, that's all."

"Why not move to another town? Stay here. You don't have to go back to Earth."

"I don't have to, but I want to."

"Don't you see how this looks, Hugh? He bullied you, and you're folding up."

"Bruce, Pella, why don't you round everybody up, take the ice cream out back, let us talk," said Joe Kincaid, waving his hands vaguely at the watchful children.

"If you want to get rid of us, don't use *that* stuff as a bribe," said Bruce. "And quit calling it ice cream."

"I really can't stay," said Hugh Merrow. "I should get back and help. I have to crate up the canvases myself."

"You came to talk about this," said Clement. "So stay and talk."

"I came to let you know about it," said Merrow, backing toward the door. "And thank you. That's all."

"You'd be thanking us better if you stayed and fought—"

"I'm not interested in staying just for the sake of a

point. Again—thank you, Clement. Joe, Ellen." Merrow's eyes flicked over to Pella and Bruce, then away, seemingly unsure whether the silent children were his allies or his oppressors. "Goodbye."

The hilarity was gone from the Southport ice cream. Now they all picked at the feeble dessert in grim, unspoken agreement that it was awful. Clement left the table first, and took the chair Raymond had taken before, the sulking chair. Pella recognized his expression. It said Clement was wrestling with notions beyond any grasp beside his own.

One more future voter gone, Pella thought, before she lapsed into a sleep so deep that someone—Clement? Joe?—had to carry her home.

Fifteen

"Sit still," said the Archbuilder named Lonely Dumptruck to Martha Kincaid.

Hugh Merrow was gone, and three Archbuilders—Lonely Dumptruck, Hiding Kneel, and Gelatinous Stand—had claimed his house and were painting over his abandoned canvases. Today Gelatinous Stand was posing for Hiding Kneel, and Martha Kincaid was posing for Lonely Dumptruck. The two models were perched on stools, side by side, in front of the open window. The sky behind them was yellow and pink.

"I'm thirsty, though," said Martha Kincaid through clenched teeth, squirming on the stool where she sat. Her pose included a fixed smile, which grew increasingly pained and artificial.

Bruce Kincaid and Raymond were making lemonade, blending packets of powdery crystals into a pitcher of water from Hugh Merrow's tap. "Just a minute," said Bruce. "We'll bring you some."

Morris Grant and David Marsh pawed through the closet like happy animals, examining the things Hugh Merrow had left behind, the books, the piles of drawings and notebook jottings, the scraps of clothing. Pella sat by herself at Hugh Merrow's table, listening to the chatter. She felt calm among the other children. Her presence had reunified the group. They'd gathered Raymond back in, so he wasn't out in the valley, elaborately mourning his mother.

She resisted going out to her hiding place, though it pulled at her, like sleepiness, or David's need to watch television back when they lived in Brooklyn, an urge just to be watching, not caring what show was on.

Household deer flitted through the corners of the house. Pella ignored them, too.

Bruce brought Pella the first poured glass of lemonade, favoring her as he always did. The drink still whirled from being stirred, a tiny galaxy of grains at the bottom of the glass.

Martha climbed off her stool to take her glass, obviously happy for an excuse to break the pose.

"Lonely Dumptruck's not done painting you, Martha," said Bruce.

"I'm tired." She gulped at the lemonade, brow furrowed. "I don't want to pose anymore."

"I will pose and you may paint," said Lonely Dumptruck to Martha.

"Okay," said Martha, brightening. "That's what I wanted to do anyway."

The canvas already featured Hugh Merrow's sketch

of an Archbuilder in a wash of umber and turpentine. The Archbuilder had gone over it with thick globs of red and black to mark out the dark of Martha's hair and eyes, then worked with white paint and a palette knife to depict Martha's teeth.

Now Lonely Dumptruck mounted the stool by the window, and Martha, holding her glass of lemonade in her left hand, took up a brush in her right and swirled the red and black and white paint into a brownish orb.

"Chocolate pie!" she said delightedly.

"Lonely Dumptruck," corrected Hiding Kneel, breaking concentration on its own painting, and looking over at Martha's work. "Not Chocolate Pie."

Hiding Kneel's portrait of Gelatinous Stand was completely abstract, as far as Pella could tell. It involved a lot of blue.

"Oh, come *on,*" said Raymond. "Don't tell me there's an Archbuilder named Chocolate Pie."

"Why not?" said Bruce. "They'll use anything for a name. In English, anyway."

"English is a language all of names," said Hiding Kneel.

"What's that supposed to mean?" said Raymond.

Pella reached the bottom of her lemonade, and accidentally sipped in a sludge of sugary dregs. She spit it back into the glass.

"They think English is funny," said Bruce, trying to be helpful. "Don't you, Kneel?"

"English words are funny," said Hiding Kneel. "English sentences are grave."

"Like to bury people?" said Martha. She was mixing paints together on the palette, making more brown out of the bright colors.

"Not that kind of grave," said Bruce.

"Me and Ray saw a dead body once," said David, emerging from the closet with a stack of Hugh Merrow's books tipped back against his chest. "At Coney Island. Tell them, Ray."

"You didn't even want to look at it," said Raymond. "It made you cry."

"I did not cry."

"Yes, you did," said Raymond. "You cried and ran."

Morris Grant stepped out of Hugh Merrow's closet, and jostled at the pile of books in David's arms from behind so they toppled and scattered on the floor.

"Cut it out," said Pella. She wanted Raymond and David to change the subject. The day at the beach was the day of Caitlin's first seizure.

We saw *two* dead bodies at Coney Island, Pella thought.

David left the books where they'd fallen. Morris kicked one so it skidded across the floor, toward the painters. A household deer scampered out of the way. Hiding Kneel put down his paintbrush and picked up the book, and began reading.

"Quit," said Bruce to Morris.

"Give me some lemonade," said Morris, grinning like a creature that lived on reprimands.

Bruce frowned, but poured him a glass.

"Lonely pie, lonely chocolate pie," Martha was saying to herself under her breath as she mixed the paint.

"But what was your name before you learned English?" said Raymond to Hiding Kneel. It was an obvious question. She wondered why she hadn't thought of it.

"Hiding Kneel Before English," said Hiding Kneel.

"That can't be right," said Bruce to the Archbuilder. "What Raymond means is—"

They were interrupted by the appearance of a figure in the doorway. Doug Grant. He surveyed the room—the painters and models, the lemonade drinkers around the table, Pella—and stepped inside.

"What's all this?" he said.

"Hugh Merrow left a lot of stuff behind," said Bruce. "The Archbuilders wanted to paint, so they kind of moved in."

"Huh."

"Older Grant, Hello," said Hiding Kneel. "Are you interested in making a mark in paint?"

"No thanks," said Doug Grant. He nudged the books on floor with his shoe. "I bet you could sell some of this stuff to Wa."

"It's mostly crap," said Morris.

"Want some lemonade?" said Raymond.

"Sure."

Raymond poured him a glass. Doug drank it standing in the middle of the room, Adam's apple bobbing furiously, chin wet. Lonely Dumptruck and Gelatinous Stand retook their poses, and Martha and Hiding Kneel returned to their painting.

"Hey, Pella Marsh," said Doug Grant, staring from behind his glass.

"What?" she said.

"I've noticed you," he said.

"So?" said Pella.

She wondered if saying her whole name came from Efram. Did Efram talk about her?

"Noticed me what?" she said.

"Not noticed doing," said Doug Grant. "Just noticed."

Morris, agitated, threw a book at David. It missed, clattered to the floor.

"Your little brother's a pain," said Bruce to Doug.

"I know," said Doug, talking like Morris wasn't there.

"A pain," said David tauntingly to Morris. "A pain in the rain."

"Paint in the rain," echoed Martha absently, as she concertedly pushed her brown smudge to every corner of the canvas.

"Why don't your mom and dad tell him to cut it out?" said Bruce, not letting it go. "Why don't they ever show their faces in this town anyway?"

"You ought to mind your own business, Bruce," said Doug. He finished his lemonade and put the glass on the table.

"Isn't a town," said Morris.

"We could show their faces in this town that isn't a

town," said Hiding Kneel. "We could paint their faces and show them."

"Paint their faces, paint their faces in the rain," said Martha.

"Well, I just think somebody should tell Morris something," said Bruce to Doug, a little petulantly.

"You tell him what you want to tell him," said Doug, looking surprisingly miserable. It struck Pella that she had something in common with Doug Grant. Like her, he was stranded between adults and children.

But he was dangerous, like a part of Efram scraped raw, all nerve and fury.

A household deer stumbled on a book, and did a neat somersault, then flickered into a corner. The room was still, except for the scraping of paintbrushes.

Doug went to the door. "Come on, Morris. Why do you want to hang out with these kids that don't even like you?"

"Shut up," said Morris. He was drawing in a book.

"There aren't any *other* kids," said Raymond.

"I like him," said David.

Pella wanted to shift into the nearest household deer and scurry away.

"Well, I'm going," said Doug. He'd plainly wanted more of a reaction. But the group of children and Archbuilders was too placid, too imperturbable. It took an outsider to show how much of a group they'd become, each with their place. Even Morris.

"Might you consider sitting for a portrait, older Grant?" said Hiding Kneel. "I hope to create a town gallery comprised of such."

"Isn't any town," said Morris.

Doug peered at the Archbuilder's painting. "You don't need models to paint like that," he said. "See you later."

"See you, Doug," said Bruce.

"Any town in the rain," sang Martha, dashing a streak of green across her brown orb.

Pella followed Doug Grant outside, but he'd already slipped off, trackless, into the valley. She imagined him wandering, a knot of gnarled anger out under the sun, strange to himself. His ugly solitude somehow inspired her.

So she wandered away. She went to her hiding place.

A minute later she was running, a household deer.

First she looked for Doug, fanning out in the direction of Efram's, crisscrossing the valley. But he'd disappeared. He had a knack for that. She wondered if he had a hiding place of his own, a turret or hole.

Leading two other deer, she doubled back, to look in at Hugh Merrow's. Bruce and Raymond were painting now. Pella guessed they'd both been shy to paint in front of her. Lonely Dumptruck was posing for Bruce, Gelatinous Stand for Raymond. Hiding Kneel was seated at the table, reading one of Hugh Merrow's books. Martha was dancing around the edge of the room, still singing to herself. Morris and David were painting on the wall.

She darted off. One of the other deer stayed,

slipping through Merrow's door. The other followed her.

She hurried away from the houses now, out into the empty valley, where deer bounded together and apart, like runners in some goalless relay. Like dancing skeletons in the sun. Pella lost herself in the frivolous, hectic chase.

One deer was rounding up the others, running tight circles. It was a spying call. The deer had found something to look at. The deer that was Pella did its best to ignore it, circling out of the gathered groups, hiding in dusty collapsed towers.

The rounding-up deer took a group of four others out in the direction of the lesbians' house, then returned and rounded up some more. The Pella-deer watched from a patch of shade, twitching, attentive. She was spying despite herself, spying on the other household deer.

The rounding-up deer was goofy, unsteady on its feet. It bumped into the others, tripped, then dizzily bounded back to its feet. But it knew what it wanted. It kept gathering others, leading them over the ridge. Soon the valley was empty.

Pella-deer's curiosity won out.

The yard of the lesbians' house was empty. Pella-deer was confused. There had been so many deer headed that way. Wherever they were being led, some number should have split off from the group to spy here. Could they be inside? She went inside to look.

The front room and kitchen were also empty of deer. Llana Richmond stood at the table, chopping vegetables. Julie Concorse lay on the couch, reading. Their baby wasn't in the room. Pella-deer scouted the four corners of the front room, found one deer dozing under the couch. She gave it a thump with her twiggy hind leg and darted away, irritated by the mystery.

Her answer lay in the baby's room. Melissa Richmond-Concorse stood in her tiny bed, leaning over the rail, murmuring, clutching at the deer that stood nearest. The room was packed with deer. It rippled and shone like a sea with tiny liquid bodies. The deer overlapped in rows, craning their giraffe-necks to see, dashing up in alternating sprints, almost within range of the giggling, gasping child's curled fingers.

Pella-deer squeezed into the room. She understood now. The rounding-up deer had been Melissa Richmond-Concorse. The baby herself, incarnated. She wasn't taking the pills either. So when the baby napped she became a deer, one as giddy and impulsive as a two-year-old. Today the baby had stumbled out into the valley and rounded up some playmates, then returned to her baby-self to admire them.

The room whirled with tiny figures, but the only sound was Melissa's gurgling. Pella could hear the clank of dishes and the murmur of conversation from the kitchen. Llana Richmond and Julie Concorse were oblivious. The deer didn't even rustle, just flowed silently, like underwater creatures. One deer, two deer, red deer, blue deer, thought Pella. She wanted to get near the baby too. It was like a chance to step into a picture-book world, where hide-and-seek had only to do with a delight in faces hidden and uncovered, where it had no moral dimension, no measure of guilt. The opposite of the adult spying she detested.

Sixteen

"Do you want to go for a walk?" said Diana Eastling.

"I guess," said Pella.

Clement was in the kitchen. When Pella came home he'd announced preemptively that Diana Eastling was coming for dinner. "Just like you wanted," he told Pella. She'd made a face at him. His secret wants were more the point, surely. Pella didn't have any interest in Diana Eastling now.

But that didn't matter, since here she was.

They went out onto the porch. The sun was going down. "Where?" said Pella.

"Doesn't matter," said Diana Eastling. "Just a walk."

Pella and Diana Eastling strolled out into the wastes behind the homestead. The household deer seemed to be running in slow motion, their elongated shadows vibrating like plucked strings across the dust.

"What's happening to you?" said Diana Eastling.

"To me?"

"To your body."

Did she mean Pella's small asymmetrical breasts? No. "Nothing," said Pella.

"Nothing Archbuilderish?" said Diana Eastling. "Nothing at all?"

The jocular and generous tone Pella chose to ignore. "Nope." She kept a half step ahead as they walked.

"Clement says otherwise."

"What does Clement know?"

Diana Eastling didn't answer that, meaning *nothing*, as far as Pella was concerned.

And guess what I do know, she wanted to add in the silence.

"Your brother said you sleep all day," said Diana Eastling.

"Who?"

"David."

"Not all day." Pella kicked at stones in her path. She felt peevish, only half-willing to have this conversation. She wanted access to Diana Eastling's knowledge of the Planet of the Archbuilders. But any pleasure in talking was spoiled by what Pella knew about Diana Eastling and Clement.

"Do you ever dream that you're running? Out here?" Diana Eastling waved her hand to indicate the valley floor. The gesture reminded Pella of Efram.

Do I ever, thought Pella. She caught herself smiling. Then she caught Diana Eastling noticing her smile.

"Why?" said Pella. "Do you?"

She turned, and saw that Diana Eastling was smiling too.

In that moment Pella became completely unafraid of what the Archbuilder viruses might do to her. She saw that Diana Eastling believed they were harmless. So Pella could let them live in her, could follow where they led.

That was all she could possibly want from this conversation. It had come so easily. And now Pella didn't care to indulge Diana Eastling for a second more.

"Dinnertime," she said, and ran toward the house.

As soon as she'd wolfed down her dinner, a bland stew of various potatoes, Pella pulled away from the table. The others were still eating. Clement had barely begun—he was fussing around Diana Eastling, playing host. Raymond and David were arguing about Morris Grant, eating slowly to keep Clement from heaping more on their plates.

"Pella—" said Clement.

"I'm going out," she said, and went, though it was night.

In her hiding place she crouched down and pulled the blanket over herself.

She had her purpose now. To find Efram. The conversation with Diana Eastling had freed her. Now a purpose coursed in her, a fever, a song.

That viruses were so she could learn the secrets of

the one who knew everyone else's secrets. So that only she would know him. So that only she would understand him.

She felt his contempt for Clement, for Hugh Merrow, Diana Eastling, and the left-behind Archbuilders, felt it as a thrilling vibration that ran through her, an animating current. She hated everyone he hated. She and Efram had an understanding. They alone felt the meaning in the chunks of Archbuilder architecture, they alone knew the ugly truth about Hugh Merrow. For she'd seen it too, seen something terribly wrong, even if she couldn't say what it was. She'd been wrong in keeping the secret, foolish mistaking Efram for an enemy. Pella wanted to be absorbed into Efram now, wanted to live in his compound and laugh at the families, wanted to stride with exquisite bitterness inside his footsteps.

She needed to see him alone in his house. She had to spy on him once, then never again.

Her self flitted into a deer and ran across the darkened valley, exhilarated.

His windows glowed a little, like a flame through candle wax. Their small light glinted off the windows of the greenhouse, so it almost seemed the source of the light. Pella-deer dashed on tiptoe amidst the planting pots and scraps of metal, over Efram's mosaic of stones, to his door.

She listened. Nothing. Just Ben Barth's chickens in the coop behind her. She zipped over to the nearest window and nosed at the edges. No point of entry. Nor sound. The same at the next window. Pella recalled her visit inside. Had there been any household deer there? Was Efram's house sealed? She worked her way around the perimeter, edging her deer feet into window corners, testing for gaps. And listening for a sound from inside. She thought of his Archbuilder interior, the house within his house. Was he in it now, dreaming of space?

She found her way into the greenhouse, through the lacy shadows his plants made in the dark, but the way to his house though the greenhouse was sealed too. She was alone there, beating like a heart in the dark, among the cool leaves. If he was inside he was perfectly silent. She couldn't get inside to know, to see him. She ran back out through his yard, and up and over the ridge until his farm was out of sight.

He must be drinking at Wa's, she decided. So she went there, like an arrow shot silently across the valley. She darted inside easily, crowding aside two other deer at the window entrance. What she found there was Ben Barth slumped so deep in a rocking chair that he threatened to slide onto the floor. No other customers. E. G. Wa was cleaning up a spilled drink at Ben Barth's feet, humming to himself. Pella climbed up onto a shelf to watch.

"Where you goin' with that?" Ben Barth said suddenly, rolling his head.

"You're done," said Wa.

"Where—"

"You're alone," said Wa. "Sleep it off."

"Fuck."

"Go home," said Wa, suddenly fierce.

"I don't have a home," said Ben Barth.

"Well, who's fault is that?" said Wa. "You oughtta take over Hugh Merrow's homestead."

"Hah!"

"What's so funny?" said Wa.

"Place is overrun with Archbuilders," mumbled Ben Barth.

"They'll go if you clear 'em out," said Wa.

"Huh," said Ben Barth, and he seemed to lapse into himself again.

"Come on," said Wa. "I'm closing early tonight."

Pella slipped outside. She didn't want to see more. The scene disturbed her. What was Ben Barth doing drunk so early in the night? Where was Efram?

Something was wrong tonight.

A trio of household deer ran past her, toward Hugh Merrow's place.

A high column of flame climbed up through the top of the house like an Archbuilder tower, visible across the valley before she was close enough to see the house itself, though when she joined the ring of household deer that stood watching Hugh Merrow's home burn Pella saw that parts of it were only just catching fire. The door was open. Pella crept as near as she could. The fire smelled like garbage, like rotting food. The far wall, still unburned, was covered with roasting canvases. They smoked black and brown before bursting like bloated stomachs with fire. Merrow's palette table was sitting in the middle of the floor. Martha and Bruce and Raymond and David had squeezed out tube after tube of paint onto the table, and now the wet gobs of pigment were hissing and popping, boiling in garish purple and turquoise flame.

Then Pella saw it, underneath the table. The Archbuilder, lying still, its fur dull from the fire.

She thought for a moment that its tendrils were moving. They *were* moving, not alive, but curling in the heat. The floorboards underneath it were smoldering. Then flames consumed the head of the Archbuilder entirely.

Nothing was alive in the fire except the fire itself.

The heat floated out in waves, making its own wind in the still, cool night. Pella staggered backward on her tiny legs, almost blown over. She was stunned by the fury of the fire. It roared like a being, roared for an answer. There was no one there to give it one. Only household deer. Which was the same as nobody. Pella herself felt insufficient to the fire, and the other deer were less, were nothing. They were air, smoke, virus. Nobody was seeing this, nobody could.

Pella couldn't see the Archbuilder anymore. She thought, Terrible things happen when nobody is looking. When I am looking. She fled.

Dear Miss Marsh,
I believe you left these at my house.

Efram Nugent

The note was attached to the bag of pills, which was set inside the entrance of her hiding place. Pella saw it when she woke. Her real body felt huge to her, thick and numb compared to the sliver of being that witnessed the fire. But she trembled just as fiercely as she had as a deer.

Efram knew where she hid. Like Bruce before, he'd been here while she was asleep. He'd seen her dreaming body.

And he was out tonight, in the time since she'd come to her burrow. He'd been out in the valley, roaming around.

Seventeen

"Pella, wake up."

She opened her eyes. It was David.

"Clement said you would get me breakfast," he said.

"Where's Clement?"

"There's a meeting."

"What kind of meeting?"

"Because of the fire."

The night came back, the burning house. She sat up. "Where's Raymond?"

David shrugged. "You know Diana Eastling stayed in Clement's room all night?"

"Get out of here," Pella said. "I have to get dressed."

When David left the room Pella took the bag of pills out from under the bed. Without pausing to think she put two of them in her mouth and swallowed. They stuck. She reached for the glass of water by her bed and washed down the pills, gulping away the lump in her throat, then took a third and swallowed it, too.

No more spying. No more fire.

Let Clement be right and Efram be wrong. Or let them both be wrong now. Let them both be her enemy.

She dressed and went outside. The day was windy and hot, as if the Archbuilder weather had shaped itself after the fire.

The ones she would have expected were there, the Kincaids, E. G. Wa, Ben Barth, and Doug Grant. But the lesbians were there too, Llana Richmond holding their baby. And Snider and Laney Grant. People she never saw away from their homes, people she never saw unless she slipped through their windows, invisible. They stood or sat awkwardly in the Kincaids' living room, listening to Clement, in postures of defeat or barely suppressed panic, betraying their reluctance at being gathered. Only Diana Eastling was missing. And Efram, of course.

Pella moved inside and closed the door, leaving David on the porch with the other children. Clement glanced at her and went on. Pella saw the shine in his eyes, saw the outlines of his imaginary podium. Spend the night with Diana Eastling, Pella thought, then wake to a crisis. Lucky Clement.

Pella found a spot and slumped down against the wall, tucking her knees up, making herself small. Doug Grant glared at her. He was there on Efram's behalf, Pella knew, not as part of Clement's meeting. He stood near the door, eyes wild, jaw pulsing under his cheek, looking on the verge of twisting in half out of sheer fury.

"I suggest you walk out and get a good look," Clement was saying. "A few hours before it burned all our kids were in that house playing," said Clement. "Not just Archbuilders. Though why Archbuilders should be any less a part—"

"That's why it's good it burned," said Doug Grant jaggedly. "Let them come out into the open, not hide in Hugh Merrow's old place—"

"Shut up, Dougie," said Snider Grant. He looked at the floor while he spoke, and ran the back of his hand across his mouth. "What do you have to say about it?"

Snider Grant talks just like Morris, Pella thought. A drunk is the same as an unpopular boy.

Snider's wife Laney Grant stood immobile beside her husband, arms wrapped around herself.

"You want these people to think you did this thing?" Snider Grant said, still not looking at his son.

"Nobody thinks you did it," said Clement.

"Sure," said Doug Grant. "You think Efram did." He went to the door. "Screw you all," he said, looking at his father. He went out.

Clement didn't even glance after him. "There's a decision to make," he went on. "We need to get some answers. We can be intimidated and disorganized or we can begin to act like a community."

He was talking past them, Pella saw. Over their heads, to a distant back row that didn't exist. He was talking to history.

"What does that mean?" said Julie Concorse. She was oblivious to history. "What do you want to do?"

"I think we ought to go out and talk to Efram Nugent, as a group," said Clement.

"Great," said Ellen Kincaid bitterly. "Go and form a posse, just like Efram did with Hugh Merrow. That's great. You have about as much evidence as he did, too."

"Ellen—" said Joe Kincaid.

"Let me talk, Joe. I don't see why you can't— where's Diana Eastling? Why don't you get her? She can talk to Efram. She knows him."

Pella was sick of hearing about Efram and Diana Eastling. She hated Diana Eastling.

The wind outside was rattling the windows.

"She wouldn't come," said Clement. He wound down, suddenly out of energy. "I agree, she should be here. She doesn't want anything to do with it."

The door opened. It was Bruce, Martha, David, Morris Grant. "Can we come in?" said Bruce. "It's kind of dusty out." As he spoke the wind tipped over a bucket on the porch, which rolled, clanging, until it came to rest against the house.

The lesbians' baby began crying.

"Get inside," said Ellen Kincaid, weary now. "Close the door." She placed her palms on Bruce's and Martha's heads. David and Morris sat together by the door. Looking at Clement, Ellen Kincaid said, "For God's sake, send one person, someone who knows Efram. Don't act like a mob."

The room turned its whole attention spontaneously to Ben Barth. He sat propped against a windowsill, as slumped and beaten-looking as the night before, at Wa's. He didn't move to acknowledge their attention.

"We won't act like a mob," said E. G. Wa. "We won't because we don't agree what needs doing."

"Gathering doesn't make a mob," said Clement feebly. "A community has a right to hold a meeting."

Ben Barth curled further into himself and emitted a little moan of displeasure. Pella thought of the day she'd first met Ben Barth. He'd been so excited by the new family's arrival on the Planet that he couldn't shut up. Now he was like a guilty shred of himself, suffering the weight of the accusations that Efram never even seemed to notice.

The wind shook the house. Pella looked up with a start at a thump outside. The bucket, or something else, blown off the porch. Melissa Richmond-Concorse cried louder.

"March us across to Efram's farm and see if he thinks it's a meeting," said Ellen Kincaid. "I'm sorry, Clement. It doesn't make sense to me."

"Not without proof," said Julie Concorse. "I agree."

"Nobody saw anything?" said Joe Kincaid. "Nobody knows what happened?"

Why hadn't she taken the pills sooner? Just a day would have been enough. To be asleep, truly asleep in her bed. Not to have known the fire. Not to be the witness.

Or could the urge to spy be stopped by the pills that quickly, in just a day? Pella felt a thread of fear inside her. What if nothing stopped it once it started, no matter how many pills you took? She wanted to run home and swallow another one.

When she looked up again Efram had come in.

He held the door open for a moment and pointed outside. "Feel that wind?" he said.

Nobody spoke. The sky was yellow, the wind shrill.

He closed the door. "There's a pollen storm coming," he said. "You people ought to make sure your homes are sealed up."

Pella stared from her spot on the floor. Had he seen her? She looked away, not wanting to feel his stony presence looming.

"Pollen storm?" said Llana Richmond.

Wa spoke eagerly. He seemed grateful to have the meeting broken. "Stuff blows around all of a sudden. When the potato vines are full of seeds. So the potatoes get in all kinds of nooks and crannies. Get in your house if you aren't careful. Find them growing in the toilet."

"We need to talk to you, Efram," said Clement.

"So I heard," said Efram. "I'm here. Talk."

"It's about the thing that happened out there, Efram," said Joe Kincaid. "At Hugh Merrow's place."

"Let's go," said Laney Grant in a panicky, whining voice. She grabbed at her husband's arm. He shrugged her away childishly, then followed her to the door. Morris Grant glared at his parents' backs. The wind kicked pebbles across the porch, past the open door. One rattled in across the floorboards before Snider Grant closed the door.

Pella noticed there weren't any household deer around.

"The thing that happened," repeated Efram. "You mean the fool Archbuilder that started a fire and got itself killed?"

He made it sound like the title of a fable, Pella thought. Another little play he was going to put on for them, a lesson.

"There always were a lot of volatile ingredients sitting around Hugh Merrow's place," said Efram, with a hint of satisfaction. "Somebody should have gone in there and cleaned up, maybe this wouldn't have happened."

"Come on, Efram," said Joe Kincaid. "Archbuilders don't burn down buildings."

Efram raised his eyebrows. "Too bad we don't have a chance to ask Truth Renowned why it made an exception to your rule, Joe."

"That was Truth Renowned?" said Clement nervously.

"I talked to Gelatinous Stand and Lonely Dumptruck just now," said Efram. He jerked his thumb over his shoulder, indicating the valley. The places Clement knew nothing about. "All three of them spent the last couple of nights at Merrow's, but they were out when Truth Renowned started the fire."

So Efram had already spoken to the Archbuilders about the fire. Clement's questions were all anticipated.

The energy in the room drained toward Efram. Clement was lost. Pella thought irrationally that it was too early in the morning for such a total defeat. The rest of the day spread before them, crushed. The rest of their lives on the planet. Where could Clement go from here?

When he lost his election he should have died, not Caitlin. Died and spared them this.

The wind outside was shaking the windows.

"Efram," said Clement softly.

"What?" said Efram. His eyes were searching the room restlessly, but they still hadn't lit on Pella. She might as well have been a household deer as her real self, for all Efram cared.

And he might as well be a killer and liar, a fire starter, for all she cared.

"Some of us want to learn to live with Arch-builders," Clement said. He picked the words one by one, as though he knew his thread was very thin. "Work together with them, make a town."

Efram scowled. "Don't let me stand in your way," he said. "Only if you don't get home soon and close your windows you'll be in charge of a potato factory, not a town."

"Efram's got a point about the pollen storm—" began Joe Kincaid.

"Things are changing," Clement went on, in some speechifying trance now, back for a moment on his podium, though it might be invisible to anyone but Pella. "Some of us want to come to a real understanding of their culture and biology instead of resisting it, being suspicious and superstitious about it—"

"Be more specific, Mr. Marsh," said Efram. "Some of us have a good understanding of the Archbuilders."

"There are families here who aren't taking the antiviral drugs," said Clement. "We'd like to see what happens if we open ourselves to the Archbuilder viruses—"

"We?" said Efram, raising his eyebrows, interested at last.

Clement nodded at Llana Richmond and Julie Concorse. The baby Melissa was sitting at Llana Richmond's feet now, playing with her shoelaces. "More than just one family," he said.

"How do you know what we're doing?" said Julie Concorse fiercely.

"Mr. Wa mentioned it," said Clement. "I don't know of any other source for the pills, outside of Southport—"

"I didn't mean to poke into your business," said Wa pleadingly.

"It's not your fault," said Llana Richmond. She looked at Clement. "Don't drag us into your battles, Marsh."

Efram stood by silently, radiating impatience, letting Clement's gesture crumble in dissension.

Meanwhile, the wind was rising.

Clement looked half-asleep now, even standing on his feet. There was a dumb hint of a smile on his face. He'd collapsed into himself. One by one the others had left, stepping out into the howling wind, first Efram, taking

Ben Barth with him back to his farm, then E. G. Wa, then Julie Concorse and Llana Richmond, with their baby. Morris had asked if he could stay there, at the Kincaids', to wait out the storm, and he and Bruce and Martha had followed Ellen Kincaid into the back room, stranding Pella and David with Joe Kincaid and Clement.

"Clement," said Joe Kincaid gently. "You really do want to be indoors when it hits."

Clement still hadn't moved. Pella got up from the floor and took his hand, took David's, led them to the door. They ducked their heads into the wind and headed for home.

Poor Clement, she thought. Always right, and always wrong.

David sat at the table. Pella brought out a loaf of Ellen Kincaid's bread from the cupboard and set David to slicing it and spreading mustard on the slices. Then Pella got out the cheese and turkey and she and David assembled sandwiches, a pile of them, cut into triangles. Clement and Raymond didn't come out of their rooms. Pella and David sat in silence at the window, eating and watching the potato-vine pollen swirl in the air and batter gently against the house.

Bruce and Martha and Morris were waiting for them after the storm, when Pella and Raymond and David went out wonderingly into the valley. They fell into step together, headed out past Wa's, away from their homes. They all were quiet, even Bruce, even Morris. It was only the middle of the day, and too much had happened. The meeting at the Kincaids' seemed remote, a thing that had happened to other people, not them. Everything was in disarray. The planet had humbled them.

The pollen, which seemed to fill the sky during the peak of the storm, was invisible now, all drifted or blown into corners, under ledges. The potato vines had curled back to the ground. Their leaves were still now in the dead air. The household deer had come out of hiding, and were running insanely everywhere. Pella ignored them. She didn't feel any urge to be among them, didn't feel the sleepy curiosity calling her, didn't miss feeling it. That part of her was gone.

Without speaking Pella steered the group in the direction of her hiding place, the half-buried Archbuilder turret. The group was sheepish and easily led. They came over the ridge behind the shell that hid Pella's secret bed, and stood nearly on top of it.

"Careful," said Pella.

Martha was standing ahead of the others. Bruce took her shoulder and pulled her back. He knelt down and thumped the crust with the flat of his hand. "Yeah, it's hollow."

"What is it?" said David.

"Just some old Archbuilder building," said Morris.

"Let's knock it down," said Pella.

Bruce looked at her questioningly. Pella turned away from him. She renounced her secret life, including Bruce's conspiring glances.

Let Raymond's cache of mourning photographs be the only reverent secret hidden out in the valley.

"It's not safe," she said. "Somebody might fall in."

Morris Grant picked out the largest rock he could find and pulled it up to the level of his chest, then staggered forward and let go. The rock sank into the wall of the structure but didn't collapse it. It sat like a scab or a tumor, half-buried. Pella thought of her blanket and bottle of water that were underneath and would be entombed. Like a cradle for a baby who would never be born.

"C'mon," said Morris, "help me." Teetering out incautiously over the sunken stone, Morris began tapping at it with his toe.

"Careful," said Raymond, "you'll fall."

"Let's use rocks," said David.

Bruce looked at Pella again. She met his eyes, and shrugged.

David and Martha carried smaller stones over and dropped them on top of Morris's. Pella felt a flush of pleasure at the easy manipulation. The other children were like her arms and legs, doing what she willed them to do. Bruce joined in now, raising a flat stone over his head and plunging it into the depression that had formed in the top.

"Here," said Raymond. "Quit throwing." He sat on the edge of the hollow and brought his heels down in unison. David and Martha and Morris immediately joined him. Kicking together, they brought the shell down. It crumpled with a dusty exhalation, entombing Pella's little bed. The heap of rocks slid over the top, a tiny avalanche sealing the place that had been her entrance.

"There," said Morris with enormous satisfaction, as though he'd both conceived the project and been the one to carry it through.

"There," said David too, pretending to huff with effort.

"Let's go look at Hugh Merrow's place," said Bruce. Now he avoided Pella's eyes. "See what's left standing."

"Maybe that's unsafe too," said Morris. "Maybe we'll have to knock it down."

"Okay," said David.

"Knock it down," said Martha dreamily.

Raymond didn't speak, but like the others he seemed brightened by their destruction of Pella's hiding place.

Moving intently now, they went across the ridge at the top of the valley, to Merrow's.

What remained of Hugh Merrow's house was another crust on the verge of collapse. The blackened walls still stood, but the interior partitions and everything within them had vanished. The roof was gone. There were no traces of the canvases that Martha and Raymond and Bruce and the Archbuilders had decorated just a day before. The palette table and the easels and the chairs were all reduced to indistinguishable char, in heaps on the floor. The blackened sink stood sprouting from the well like a gnarled mushroom, the countertop burned away around it.

The body of the Archbuilder was gone. Pella wondered if Raymond or David or Martha or Morris even understood that it had been there.

She knew Bruce understood, from the way he avoided her gaze.

It was Bruce who led the attack on the skeleton of the house. He kicked in the door frame, so the wall around it began to buckle. Then he found the place where the wall sections met and began kicking. Scuffs of black soot covered his sneakers instantly. The others joined him. This time even Pella. Without fear for their safety they swarmed the ruins, tearing the walls apart with their hands and feet. The house was flimsy, like a set for a play. The front fell to Bruce's attack almost instantly. The families might as well have been sleeping outside like Archbuilders as in this joke, this wisp of a house. It deserved wrecking. Pushing together like a team of dray horses, the children brought down the whole rear wall, splaying the back of the house open, revealing the spread of broken spires on the horizon. Then they wrenched down the last of the side walls, too. The wall groaned a minor protest, then fell. Puffs of newly fallen pollen drifted out of corners where it had lodged. The floor was strewn with shards of blackened wood and the rubble of ruined items, paintbrushes, kitchenware, a few books. Ashes. The children stopped and regarded their work. The house was done. It was garbage. It belonged to the Planet now. It begged to be covered with vines. That would be mercy. The only thing standing was the sink, a feeble echo of a ruined tower.

Now they stood gathered at what had been the front door, gazing at the valley through the space of the wrecked house.

"Look," said Martha.

"What?" said Bruce.

Martha pointed out to the left. "There."

"What?" said Bruce. "There's nothing there."

"No, look," said Raymond. "She's right. Some people or something."

They all strained to see.

They wended around the flattened ruins of the burned house and down a short slope, where for a moment the distant figures were out of sight. Pella thought for a moment they'd imagined them. Then up the other side, and the figures reappeared, nearer, but still not near enough. The children walked forward, magnetized.

"Up here," said Bruce. He pointed to a rise on their left. "They won't see us."

The group scrambled after him. Pella too. She said to herself, *Spying, lying, spying, lying.* Spiers and liars.

It was three Archbuilders and Efram Nugent. They were building a sculpture in the sun. Pella recognized Hiding Kneel, Gelatinous Stand, and Lonely Dump-truck. Hiding Kneel was using a shovel to load buckets of black mud from deep under the hard floor of the valley, and the other three were packing it onto the form under construction, a figure about the size of an Archbuilder, a rough statue. Efram was working as diligently as the others, not leading them, not following. As the mud figure dried it turned the color of the rock and dust.

Then Pella saw the shoulder of the statue, where fur had been slicked down with moisture from the mud, but not covered. It was a real Archbuilder they were packing in mud. The shapes at the top were its collapsed tendrils.

"What are they doing?" said David.

"Archbuilder funeral," whispered Bruce. "Ben Barth told me about this once."

"How's it a funeral?" said Raymond.

"Like burying someone aboveground," said Bruce, not taking his eyes away. "They build the dead Archbuilder into a monument, with sticks and wire so it stands up. Sort of like, be your own tombstone."

"But what's *Efram* doing there?" said Morris.

No one had an answer for this. They stood behind Bruce on the bluff and watched as the burial party patiently slathered mud onto the still body.

Ash, fire, mud, fur, thought Pella.

"Be your own, be your own, *tomb*-stone," chanted Martha under her breath, bringing out the rhyme.

They returned to the house. Clement was gone. They were all three numbed and hungry. Pella made more sandwiches and they ate without waiting for Clement, as darkness fell.

Afterward they cleaned up the table in silence. The long day was supposed to be over now.

"Where is he?" said David at last.

"Be quiet," said Pella.

"But where is he?"

"I'll go find him. Get ready for bed."

Pella was halfway to Diana Eastling's house when she met Clement. He'd mastered this one route, at least. He could walk one path through the valley in the dark with his head down.

"Hey," said Pella, stopping him before he practically walked over her.

"Pella," said Clement, his eyes brightening momentarily, then falling.

"Where have you been?"

"Saying goodbye," he said.

"Goodbye to who?"

"Diana's leaving," said Clement. His voice was flat and dead. He trudged ahead, letting Pella fall into place beside him.

"Leaving for where?" said Pella. "Southport? Earth?"

He waved his hand carelessly behind him. The night was all around them now, the distance pressing in. "Out there. Exploring, visiting her sites. Her Archbuilder friends."

"She does that all the time."

"This is different," he said. "A long trip. She asked Raymond to watch her place for her."

"So?"

"She's getting away from me. From the town."

Pella looked over her shoulder, as though Diana Eastling might at that moment be seen skulking across the landscape. Pella had wished her away, but now she felt doomed by the loss. Diana Eastling was a thread of sanity, of control.

"Why?" said Pella.

"I tried to make her understand what Efram did, but she doesn't believe me. She says it's a grudge . . ." He broke off.

Pella decided then she'd never even seen the burning. Perhaps some household deer might have. It was likely, since household deer were everywhere. Too bad they had no voice. Too bad they had nothing to do with Pella.

"She says I'm not over Caitlin's death," Clement said. "That I'm still in love with her."

He spoke this as though the words had nothing to do with Pella, enclosing himself in the shell of his own pain, refusing the meaning of their family the way his neighbors had refused him the meaning of the town this morning.

I hope he is still in love with her, Pella thought savagely. He should be. He deserves to be.

Eighteen

In the days after the fire the valley fell into a pensive, watchful silence. The settlement, the might-be-town, was shrinking instead of growing. The spaces between things were growing instead. The silences. Diana Eastling was gone. Hugh Merrow was already forgotten, the singed scraps of his house scavenged for fuel, the ashes blown away over the wastes. New vines sprouted up everywhere out of the rubble, leaves seeking the sun, potatoes underneath, hidden, swelling in the mud. Two days after the burning Ben Barth walked into Wa's and said he was going to Southport, to work for the window maker. Alliances might be shifting, coming apart. No one asked, no one learned more. Ben Barth packed his few belongings into his battered truck and was gone by nightfall.

The Archbuilder corpse baked and rotted in the sun, untended, a desolate sculpture. Raymond began spending nights at Diana Eastling's house.

Doug Grant skulked outside Wa's.

The girl sensed something coming, some arrival or departure still unannounced. A figure on the horizon, a change in the weather. A shift or eclipse. Her family was no help. Like the not-quite-town, it was unspooled, all gaps and missed connections. The girl avoided her father, the other children, Wa's shop. She tried not to think of Efram at all. She took the pills she had stashed under her bed, two in the morning, two at night, and didn't dream, didn't wander or spy. Instead she walked out into the valley in her human body, alone, to wonder if the figure she felt moving toward her on the lonely horizon might somehow be her mother.

"I buy flour and yeast at Wa's," explained Ellen Kincaid. "Wa gets it from Southport. I buy it on my credit. Then I get eggs from Ben Barth's chickens. Same thing—I trade for finished loaves. The rest is cake and tea potatoes."

Pella and David were helping Ellen and Martha Kincaid make bread, Pella and David stirring mixtures in large bowls, while Martha was rubbing a split half tea potato around the inside of a set of pans.

A pair of household deer pottered woozily under the counter.

"Then you sell it back to Wa," said Martha.

"Just for credit," said Ellen. "No money changes hands. So we get our other groceries from him on the credit for the loaves. And other people get bread."

As Ellen Kincaid spoke her eyes grew distant, and

her voice dimmed. Why talk of *other people getting bread,* when they all felt the settlement withering?

"Also we eat a lot of potatoes," said Martha to David and Pella. "They don't cost anything."

"We eat a lot of potatoes too," said David cheerily. "And Clement buys your mom's bread."

Pella went on stirring, mashing the lumps of cake potato into the egg-and-water mixture. Ellen Kincaid poked at the charcoal through a door in the base of the oven, bunching the hot coals. A first batch of dough had risen and been distributed into six loaf pans, and now Ellen Kincaid loaded them into the upper space of the oven.

"Who's going to take care of Ben Barth's chickens now?" said Martha.

Pella whisked a handful of flour off the tabletop, in the direction of the two household deer, coating one like a powdered doughnut. It shook and ran in a circle.

"Doug Grant, I bet," said David.

"What about Doug Grant?" said Pella.

"He's helping Efram, instead of Ben," said David. "Morris told me."

Ellen Kincaid frowned. "I'm surprised Ben didn't take his chickens with him," she said. "Efram ought to take care of his own farm. If he wants chickens out there he ought to take care of them himself."

"You can't put chickens in a truck!" said Martha, delighted. "They fly away!"

"Doug Grant *wants* to live out at Efram's farm," said David. "He hates his dad."

"Shut up about Doug Grant," said Pella.

"Morris told me, that's all," said David.

Ellen Kincaid turned to the sink. "Bring that here, Pella. It needs more water." She scrubbed egg scum out of a bowl fretfully. "David, you too."

Ellen Kincaid doled out portions for each of them to knead. Pella knew they were being gently patronized. Martha's mother didn't need their help. Pella watched her knead dough, leaning into it as her hands briskly folded the stretched surfaces. David and Martha and even Pella, by comparison, were useless, mucking around, smearing bits of dough into the joints of their fingers and onto the floor. But the bread making was a little version of the town, Pella thought. The town that was supposed to be but never was. The four of them pounding and folding together Wa's flour and Efram's eggs and Archbuilder cake potatoes. It was the closest anyone had come.

"It feels like penis," said Martha. She tittered.

"Shut up," said David.

"Martha," said Ellen Kincaid.

"Penis pie, with penis butter," said Martha.

"Quit!" said David, reddening.

Martha giggled.

Ellen Kincaid stepped over and tilted Martha's head up with her hand, leaving a thumb smudge of flour on her forehead. "Whose penis?" she said, in a voice that was quiet, but focused like a beam of light.

Pella held her breath, waiting for Martha to answer. She felt Ellen Kincaid's fierce protective attention. This is what a mother does, Pella thought.

"David's!" shrieked Martha, and laughed harder.

"Be quiet!" said David.

"That's enough, Martha," said Ellen Kincaid, loudly and easily now, the moment past. "We're trying to make bread here. Take the funny stuff outside."

"But I'm *helping*. I don't want to—"

"Go."

Slumping her head from shoulder to shoulder, Martha went to the front door and out onto the porch. Daylight flooded the damp yeasty kitchen.

Ellen Kincaid put her powdery hand on David's head now. "Don't let Martha upset you."

"Sometimes I hate her," said David ruthlessly, his eyes slitted. He went on kneading his portion of dough.

Ellen Kincaid looked at Pella, her smile wry and tired and nervous at once.

Martha edged back inside while the new loaves went into the oven. The two deer danced out as she came in, one still dusted with white. Ellen Kincaid slipped the first batch of loaves out of the pans and onto cooling racks, then cut one into fat, steamy slices and slathered the slices with potato jam. David and Martha and Pella ate silently, reduced to grateful, gnawing cubs by the hot, achingly sweet bread. Ellen Kincaid watched them eat.

Afterward they bagged the loaves in plastic, and twisted the bags closed. "Here," said Ellen Kincaid, giving David and Pella each a loaf. "Take these home to your father."

"We can buy them at Wa's," said Pella, confused.

"No, take them," said Ellen, smiling sadly. "Please."

• • •

Clement was watering under his bed when they came in. He hadn't secured the window to his bedroom on the day of the pollen storm. Just as Efram had warned, the potato vines were sprouting indoors, under his bed. So Clement watered them. For the past few days he'd been obsessed with gardening, fastidiously nurturing his tiny struggling plants, both inside and outside the house.

"Why not?" he'd said to Pella when she first found him tending the sprouts. "Everyone else can go hacking them out of the ground, and we'll have our own supply right here. It's perfectly reasonable. We'll show Efram Nugent that everything doesn't have to be done his way." As if Efram would ever bother to look under Clement's bed, or be impressed to find potatoes growing there if he did. But Pella hadn't said anything then, and she didn't say anything now. Water trailed out along the floorboards toward her feet, trickling into cracks where already tiny new shoots of potato vine were inching into the house. Soon Clement's indoor farm would expand from under the bed. He'd have a whole potato room. Pella and David set the loaves of bread on the table, and David said, "Where's Raymond?"

"He's ferrying stuff over to Diana's," called Clement without looking up. "He took the bicycle."

"What stuff?" said Pella.

"I don't know. Just some stuff, his stuff."

"I wish I had a bicycle," said David.

"There's only one," said Clement. "We've got the only bicycle in town." He turned and grinned at David as if this were occasion for enormous satisfaction. David didn't seem to agree. He frowned.

"You can ride it when Ray comes back," said Clement.

"It's too big for me," said David, exasperated.

"Maybe we could buy David one in Southport," suggested Pella. "We could all go."

"I want to go to Southport!" said David.

"I don't know how we'd get there," said Clement, still poking at his vines. "I don't really see what we need from Southport that Wa doesn't stock in his shop, anyway. I doubt there's any bicycles for sale."

The house was in disarray. Jars of food sat out on the counter and the kitchen table. The shelf that had been Clement's desk was heaped with bits of Archbuilder salvage, old implements and hardware and shards of pottery that Clement had dug out of the garden. His papers and laptop were gone.

David seated himself at the table. He fumbled forlornly with the plastic bag that held the fresh loaf of bread, mouthing words to himself, then looked up suddenly. "Hey!" he said. "When are we going to have school again?"

Clement got up from his knees, and went to the sink, smiling blandly. "I guess that's up to Joe Kincaid," he said. "He's the teacher."

Joe's a teacher, Wa's a shopkeeper, Snider Grant is a drunk, and what are you, Pella thought? A bedroom farmer. You lost an election and you lost a wife and you couldn't keep a girlfriend. Now Pella wished he'd married Diana Eastling. Without her, Clement was unreachable, finished. She'd been his last brush with credibility.

Then, watching her father rinse his muddy hands at the sink, Pella felt her guilt glow inside her.

It was in the shape of a small burning house.

From the ridge she watched the farm change colors with the sunset, the greenhouse become a pink-and-orange prism, the windows of the house first reflect the rust-smeared sky then darken until they were lit from within, the shadows of the chicken coop and planters and kiln stretch longer and longer across the toast-colored flagstones until they crossed the line of the fence and beyond, the whole homestead like a sundial on the face of the valley.

In an hour of watching she'd seen Doug Grant step outside once, to pour scraps of garbage into a tray in the chicken coop, then back inside. But no sign of Efram. She'd barely seen him since the day of the storm. Still, his force encompassed the days that followed the fire and the storm, just as it hung over the homestead now as she watched. Efram's power was implicit. He'd revealed his control of the valley in glimpses and asides, stepping in to thwart Joe Kincaid or Clement here and there, then withdrawing. He commanded the valley that way, and Pella. The echo of his name, spoken by others, was stronger than any voice. He ruled by abdication.

From her vantage Pella saw Raymond's bicycle tracks veering off to the right, toward his mourning corner of the settlement. She saw Ben Barth's tire marks, tracing his path away from Efram's, toward Southport. To the east, behind a rise of towers, lay the charred and flattened remains of Hugh Merrow's house. Farther out, the Archbuilder burial statue. The valley was a map of deaths and retreats.

There was a whisper of pebbles tumbling down a grade behind her, something more than household deer. She turned, expecting Efram. Instead, ambling double-jointedly up the ridge was Hiding Kneel. The Archbuilder saw Pella and bowed, tendrils flopping forward, and continued up the path. Pella felt a faint shock at being visible in her real body, her verging-past-girlhood body. She would always now. She shouldn't miss her secret intangible deer-self.

"Hail, Pella Marsh," said Hiding Kneel, stopping a few feet from her.

"Hail," Pella repeated automatically, then felt instantly stupid about it.

"Would you be observing the landscape?" said Hiding Kneel.

Pella nodded.

"My objective also," said Hiding Kneel, moving closer. Pella stared at the Archbuilder, at the shiny, fur-ringed gaps of its eyes. It nodded at her, seeming to accept her gaze. "Your family is widely dispersed tonight."

"What?"

"In passing, below, I saw Raymond Marsh also."

"What was he doing?"

"Making circles," said the Archbuilder unhelpfully. Circles of photographs to sit inside? Or circling bicycle tracks in the dust? Pella didn't bother to ask.

Hiding Kneel brushed off a flat knee-high rock and gingerly sat, uncomfortably close to Pella, and gazed out with her over the valley.

"Below is Efram Nugent's house," it said.

"Uh-huh," said Pella, trying to avoid conversation.

"Have you ever been inside it?"

She turned, surprised. "Once," she said. "Have you?"

"Ben Barth and myself often played backgammon, when Efram Nugent was traveling."

"Oh yeah."

"Ben Barth has gone."

"I know."

"Doug Grant does not enjoy backgammon," mused Hiding Kneel after a short silence. When Pella didn't say anything, it added, "Do you perhaps play?"

"No," said Pella. Seeing she was going to have to talk to Hiding Kneel about something, she said, "So you saw Efram's walls? All the Archbuilder stuff?"

"Oh, they were very beautiful. A marvelous endeavor."

"You liked it?" It seemed wrong that the Archbuilder could be so blithely approving of Efram.

"Very certainly," said the Archbuilder.

"So why don't you fix up all the wrecked stuff around here?"

"This would be . . ." Hiding Kneel stopped to

consider. "It would be to pretend a relation I do not have, to all the wrecked stuff."

"You mean it isn't yours to fix up?" Pella turned her head at a sound. A single household deer had appeared beside them on the ridge. It danced for stability in the wind.

"It isn't," agreed Hiding Kneel. "Nor is it mine to want it fixed."

Pella wasn't sure she appreciated the distinction. "You could at least make yourself a place to sleep." She thought of her own crushed Archbuilder shell. "Where do you go at night?"

"There are various places to sleep," said Hiding Kneel airily. "I go at night where I go in the daytime, but in repose."

Pella was irritated. She couldn't sort out this answer at all. Was Hiding Kneel explaining that it slept in the rocking chair at Wa's store? That was the main place it went in the daytime.

"Well, Efram thinks you're pathetic for not living up to all this stuff," she said impulsively. She waved her hand at the ruins, grandly, the way Efram would. In the valley, night was arriving, the long shadows knitting together.

"Ah," said Hiding Kneel, tendrils rustling as it nodded its head.

"You don't care?"

"Efram Nugent's love of ancestors is quite poignant."

"He hates you." Could she make it any clearer?

Hiding Kneel should be here to keep a watch for Efram, to make sure that no fires were set, no Archbuilders murdered tonight. Instead the Archbuilder had come to admire the sunset and pine for backgammon.

I'm the only one who understands, she thought hopelessly.

Hiding Kneel sat staring out at Efram's homestead, seeming not to have heard.

"He doesn't want you in the town," she said. "If he gets his way you won't be allowed around here."

"Clement Marsh is a good man," said Hiding Kneel. "It is his town I will be allowed in. His school is where I will study."

"There isn't any school," said Pella. "My father doesn't have a town for you. This is Efram's place. Clement can't make anything happen."

"I was assured he was a potent statesman."

"He's nothing without my mother." The words snuck out of her like a thread between her lips, a betraying filament that stretched back to Brooklyn, to Pineapple Street.

"Your mother?"

"She's dead."

"So you too are concerned with the superiority of your lost ancestors," said Hiding Kneel. "Hence your receptivity to Efram Nugent's valuation of the departed Archbuilders."

"Caitlin isn't my ancestor," said Pella. "She's my mother."

"Yet you speak of her as legendary, like my departed fore-cousins," said Hiding Kneel. "And Clement

Marsh, like we who remain, is correspondingly diminished. We tiptoe in the corridors of their reputation."

"So basically you agree with Efram that you're a bunch of chumps."

"Possibly," said Kneel, tilting its head humorously. "But perhaps those departed only seem greater to us because they are gone."

"You never met Caitlin," said Pella quickly, though not before she felt a sting of doubt. Was she unfair to Archbuilders? To Clement?

"I'm sorry to say, no," said Hiding Kneel, as though it might have been a real possibility.

They sat in silence, until the Archbuilder said, "Why are you so angry at your father?"

"Because he's like *you,*" she said, before she could think. Hot tears began to cover her face.

"I do not understand."

"You couldn't." She didn't herself. What did she mean? Were Clement and Hiding Kneel both helpless? Both sad?

Both good?

"Perhaps there is another reason," suggested the Archbuilder.

"Yes," said Pella. "Because he lived and Caitlin died."

"Ah," said Hiding Kneel, after thinking for a moment. "The elegance of the explanation is that it encompasses also why you are so angry at yourself."

The two of them fell silent, as darkness closed over the valley and the farm below.

Nineteen

It began two days later, in front of E. G. Wa's place, late in an empty afternoon. Pella was coming over the hill and she caught them at it. She could have been elsewhere. She only happened to see.

Doug Grant and Wa and Joe Kincaid stood over the figure in front of the store. It was Hiding Kneel, on all fours in the dust.

"Get up," said Doug Grant shrilly, pulling on Hiding Kneel's arm, his motions hectic. It was like he wanted to pull Hiding Kneel's arm off. The Archbuilder was raked in a half circle on its knees. The other two men stood tensed, not aiding Hiding Kneel, not stopping Doug Grant from his harsh useless jerking at the Archbuilder's limbs. In the bright sun the three men threw dark, liquid shadows across the rock. The Archbuilder wallowed in its shadow, like a swimmer in mud.

Pella moved down the hill toward the store. She

didn't try to keep out of sight. As she neared she saw the shine on Hiding Kneel's fur. The Archbuilder was leaking clear fluid, like glue. Bleeding. Pella stopped, a few yards away. E. G. Wa turned and saw her. Doug Grant glanced too. Then they turned back to the Archbuilder on the ground. No one spoke.

Moving roughly, but without the savagery of Doug Grant, Joe Kincaid grabbed the Archbuilder by the fur of its shoulders and hauled it to its feet. Joe Kincaid wore a hat. Beneath it his face was red and clotted with anger. Upright, Hiding Kneel staggered, but didn't protest or struggle. The Archbuilder shook its head and tendrils as if regretfully declining some polite offer or suggestion. Pella stepped forward, entranced. It was as though she'd come over the hill into an imaginary world made up of parts of the true one. The moment was unreal, the four figures in silence and sunlight barely acknowledging her.

The spell broke when Doug Grant raised his knee into Hiding Kneel's midsection. Pella heard the crack of shell. Now Joe Kincaid pulled Doug Grant away from the Archbuilder, who had doubled over without falling.

"Enough," said Joe Kincaid.

"What?" said Doug Grant, breathing raggedly.

"Marsh," said Joe Kincaid, and he pulled Hiding Kneel upright again. The fur of the Archbuilder's chest and stomach were wet. The moistened fur parted in ridges, exposing the thinness of its torso. Its mouth was open wide, as though it were moaning soundlessly.

Doug Grant and Wa turned again to look at Pella. "She doesn't care," said Wa.

"Not her," said Joe Kincaid. "We should take Kneel to Marsh. Clement. Make him see."

"Clement Marsh is a good man," said Hiding Kneel gently. Pella was shocked to hear the Archbuilder speak. She had begun to think of it as a kind of animal or plant, the way the men were destroying its body.

"Shut up," said Wa.

"We should take it to Efram's place," said Doug Grant. "He'll be back soon. Efram'll know what to do." He said to Wa, "Let me get Efram's gun."

Wa shook his head. "Don't need a gun. It'll do what we say."

"Efram Nugent is a good man," said Hiding Kneel with exactly the same intonation.

"Quiet!" said Doug Grant.

"No, we'll go to Marsh," said Joe Kincaid. His voice was heavy. It was clear they would do as he told them. Somehow he was the leader of this misshapen venture.

Pella followed the three men and the one Archbuilder to her house, pacing them a few yards behind, not bothering to hide. The men walked into the sun, heads down, ignoring her. She was sure they knew she was there. The men had fallen back into their dreamlike silence, as if acting under another hand, following some inevitable script. The hurt Archbuilder trudged along with them, not resisting, playing its part in the dream.

It wants to see Clement, Pella thought.

He was home. He was always home, now that Diana Eastling was gone. He came to the door in bare feet.

245

Pella stood to one side of the porch and watched. Clement stepped out blinking in the brightness of the day. He'd begun keeping the windows covered, to make the house a better place for the potato vines. Moist and cool. He himself seemed to be withering.

"Joe," he said.

"Where's David?" said Joe Kincaid.

"Why?" said Clement. "I don't know where he is."

Pella knew. David and Morris Grant were out in the valley together.

"He's in trouble, Clement," said Joe Kincaid. "You'd better take care of him. He and Martha and this Archbuilder—"

"Hiding Kneel," said Clement, smiling humbly. He spoke as if he were making introductions, providing helpful clarifications.

"Efram was right, Clement. We should have been more careful."

Clement squinted. "He's hurt."

"*It,*" said Doug Grant.

Clement looked at Doug Grant, puzzled.

"I caught it with your boy, Marsh," said Doug Grant urgently. "Just like Efram said. Your boy and Martha Kincaid."

"You *caught* it?" said Clement, dazedly. "I don't understand."

"My brother—" started Doug Grant.

"Efram Nugent is a good man," said the Archbuilder quietly. Nobody paid attention.

"We need to do something," said Joe Kincaid. "We need to talk."

246

Clement shook his head. "Talk about what? We don't seem to get very much done around here with talk." He blinked again. "You've hurt this Archbuilder, Joe."

"Mr. Marsh, listen—" said Wa.

"No, no," said Clement. He shook his head again. "You should go home. I've learned about this place. Everything takes care of itself. The women—Julie Concorse and what's her name?—I was wrong when I told Efram about their baby not taking the pills. They were right. There's room here for everyone. We should leave one another alone. You're making the same mistake, Joe. A mistake I for one am done making." Pella could see his impatience to be back inside, tinkering with his kitchen inventions, tending to his potatoes. The men were invisible to him, she knew.

"Listen, Clement. The Archbuilder molested my girl."

"What?" said Clement. "That's ridiculous. No, no, you can't be serious. Why would it want—"

"I talked to her."

"We need authority, Mr. Marsh," said Wa.

Clement stepped out of the doorway. Nudging Wa aside, he took Hiding Kneel's hands in his, as if courting the Archbuilder. "This is very important," he said. "Don't let them do this to you. This is your place—"

Joe Kincaid pushed Clement away, back toward the door. At the same time Doug Grant yanked the Archbuilder's arm again, pulling its hand free of Clement's clasp.

"That's enough," said Joe. "This isn't about what's

being done to *Archbuilders*. If you can't see that—I'll tell you one thing: You'd better keep your kid away from Martha, Clement. You'd better talk to David."

Clement stood holding his shoulder where Joe Kincaid had shoved him, his mouth open.

"I told you we should have gone to Efram," said Doug Grant.

Pella rushed up onto the porch, and stepped between Joe Kincaid and her father. "Go, then," she said to Doug and Joe. "Leave him alone."

"Pella," said Clement. His voice was empty.

"Go inside," she said, and pushed Clement herself. He went in, and she closed the door. She turned and faced the men. Wa was already dragging Hiding Kneel away from the porch.

"Go to Efram, you jerks," she said. "Leave Clement alone. He didn't do anything. Neither did David."

"What do you know, Pella Marsh?" said Doug Grant. He vibrated in his place on the porch, his voice trembling, his upper lip shiny with perspiration, but he didn't move toward her.

"More than you." She leaned against the door.

Joe Kincaid looked at Pella as though it were him instead of Hiding Kneel who'd been beaten and dragged in the dust. He motioned absently at Doug to follow Wa, to leave the house, without taking his numb eyes off Pella. She stared back.

"This is about Martha," he said softly.

"I don't care," said Pella. "Go away." She knew they'd take the Archbuilder, but she couldn't help that.

They were taking Hiding Kneel with them no matter what she said.

Joe turned and the strange unhappy group formed again at the foot of the porch, the three men surrounding Hiding Kneel. They slouched off in the direction of Efram's, Doug Grant the only one with any evident vitality. Doug was spring-loaded, imbalanced. He limped from sheer agitation, one leg moving faster than the other. Pella stood there with her back against the door, watching until they were out of sight.

Did she only imagine that she felt Clement's presence on the other side of the door, listening? More likely he wouldn't even seem to understand what Pella was talking about, if she later mentioned the visit to their house. She wouldn't mention it. She wouldn't bother. She gave the four another minute to get ahead, then started for Efram's along a back path.

They stuffed Hiding Kneel into Efram's ancient shed, and Doug Grant snapped shut the rusted padlock. Pella knelt behind an empty planter at Efram's gate, watching from a distance. They hadn't seen her. The sun was nearly below the horizon now, hidden in a band of clouds. The yard glowed everywhere with orange light, and as Pella peered around the edge of the planter the men and the shed were jerky black figures vibrating in the glow.

"Efram's coming back," Doug said agitatedly. "He'll know what to do."

"Let's wait in the house," said E. G. Wa.

"Can't," said Doug Grant. "I'm not allowed."

"Crap, Doug," said Wa.

"I can't help it," said Doug Grant. "That's what Efram said."

Joe Kincaid stood to one side. He looked like he might sink into the ground under the weight of his own despair, the pressure of his crimes, his failures.

His accomplices rattled on, oblivious.

"I've known Efram a hell of a lot longer than you, Doug," said Wa. "I've *been* in his house."

"Well," said Doug Grant, slanting his jaw back and forth.

Joe Kincaid finally raised his hand to silence them. "I have to go," he said. "My daughter—my family."

Doug Grant slapped him on the shoulder. "You go. We'll keep the Archbuilder. Don't worry."

Wa nodded. Joe Kincaid turned and started for the gate. Pella shrank deeper into the shadow of the planter, but she couldn't hide. She was girl-sized, human. As Joe Kincaid opened the gate he saw her. Their eyes met for a moment, and he nodded, his expression dark, then went past without speaking.

It was as though he wanted Pella to be his own departed conscience.

Then he was gone. Pella looked around the side of the planter. Doug Grant and E. G. Wa had gone into Efram's house, leaving the padlocked shed alone.

Pella worked her way around the back of Efram's farm until she could climb the fence without being spotted. She wished she could flit into a deer body, and creep through Efram's compound unseen. Here at last was a purpose.

She might still be able, if she tried. She felt the gift was still with her, buried. But there wasn't anywhere to hide and sleep. Not out in the open, so close to Efram's, not with Doug Grant and Wa and soon Efram himself around. Anyway, she needed to be able to talk to Hiding Kneel, to find out what really happened.

The shed was shabby, made of scraps. Pella wondered if it could be brought down as easily as Hugh Merrow's house. But that had taken fire. She put her hands and weight against it. It felt solid, planted. Possibly Efram's farm was the place where human buildings grew into the ground, knitted together with the Planet, and became permanent. The shed door was open an inch, despite the lock. It was too dark inside for her to see. She knelt down by the corner of the door. She imagined she could smell the hurt Archbuilder, a sour smell.

"Hiding Kneel?" she whispered. The words were odd in her mouth. She'd never before called an Archbuilder by its name. She said the name again, a bit louder.

"Is that Pella Marsh?" said Hiding Kneel from inside, too loudly.

"Yes. Be quiet."

"I've been abducted, Pella Marsh."

"I saw."

"Joe Kincaid is a good man."

"Well, I guess. So what's he got against you?"

"Very poor information," said Kneel, sighing. For

the first time the Archbuilder's voice seemed apprehensive.

"Information?" said Pella. Looking up, she saw two figures at Efram's rear window. She drew herself around the corner of the shed, out of sight of the window.

"Morris Grant and myself," said Kneel. "We shared a lesson in observation—"

"I don't think they care what you were doing with Morris," said Pella, frantic with impatience. "Joe and Doug were talking about Martha and my brother, something happened—"

"Doug Grant is a good man."

"Not everyone is a good man, Hiding Kneel," said Pella, exasperated. She had to understand what happened. Why was the Archbuilder talking about Morris Grant?

What was a *lesson in observation?*

There was only silence from inside the shed. Pella imagined the Archbuilder lying in the dark bleeding—or oozing—to death, proclaiming the goodness of various men to the very last breath.

"Hiding Kneel—" she started, then stopped. She heard a crunching of heavy footsteps nearby, turned her head to see. The house was still. She looked back.

Efram was standing over her, hands on his hips.

"Miss Marsh," he said.

She stared up at him, from a vantage so low that she might as well have been a household deer. She felt as voiceless.

"There's a front door to my house," he said. "You're welcome to use it when you visit."

"Doug said you weren't here."

"Well I am."

"They're in your house," she said dumbly.

He reached down. Helplessly, she took his hand. His clasp was gentle for a moment, then he jerked her to her feet by her arm. She almost stumbled against him. To avoid it she staggered back against the shed door. He dragged her away from the shed.

"I don't need you to tell me who's in my house," he said.

"What about Hiding Kneel?" she said, defiantly, finding her real voice, her face hot. "You know about that?"

He didn't answer. Instead he pulled her past the house, toward the gate. His hand was dry and firm, and huge. In its grasp hers felt like something raw and newborn, all moist and soft. Pella broke into a skipping run to keep from being dragged. A pair of household deer scrambled out of their path. As fast as Efram walked, he seemed deeply unhurried, unafraid. Only a little distracted, as if reminded of some greater purpose, something mislaid.

He took her through the gate before letting go of her hand. Even then he strode on without turning to see that she was following. She did follow. The glow of the sky behind them reflected on far-off spires and hillsides. Elsewhere the valley was succumbing to the heavy, silent evening. Efram slowed enough that she could keep up with him without feeling hurried, childish. In a minute they were out of sight of his farm or any of the other homesteads, in an open, dishlike portion of the valley, like the one where she'd first seen him, coming over a hill. And there he stopped. The light around them was perfectly equal, casting no shadows, dimming steadily. She felt she couldn't stand to be near him if it were dark. If it were night.

"What did you want to talk to me about?" said Efram. "Something about an Archbuilder?"

"The one in your shed," said Pella. Her voice wavered. "You know about it."

"That's right," said Efram. "I was already home when the four of you turned up."

"I wasn't with them."

"My apologies," he said, grinning. "Creeping along behind, I should have said."

"What are you going to do?"

"Find out what happened." He stood towering, his arms crossed, smirking at her.

"From Doug Grant?"

"If that's who knows." He made it sound as orderly as that, another piece of business in the world that only he knew how to carry off sensibly.

"He doesn't know anything. He's just trying to be like you."

"Is that right. What about you? Who are you trying to be like?"

"Fuck you," she said. The flush of blood went through her whole body now.

"Go home, Pella Marsh." He raised his heavy arm

like a banner and gestured in the direction of Clement's potato-filled house.

"I can go where I want."

"Fair enough. So where do you want to go?"

She hated his confident, empty questions. She wanted to attack him, to butt her head against his stomach and push him into the dust. She wanted to feel her weight beat against him. Then, distantly, she thought again of Hiding Kneel. In the shed, in the dark. That was how she would end, she thought.

It had grown dark enough that Efram was a faceless shape in front of her now, a part of the horizon, a craggy ruin. She could no more bring him down with her to the ground than topple the ragged monoliths in the distance, or shake apart the shed that imprisoned the Archbuilder. She felt herself throb like a tiny nerve or spark, a thing that coursed harmlessly over the surface of the world.

Without speaking she turned and ran.

She'd never approached the Grants' house except as a deer. It looked the same as the others, but to Pella, seeing it under the pall of her awareness of the family, it was a gothic castle, a house in a nightmare. She shook off her fear and went to the door.

It was a while before Laney Grant answered the knock. Her face was already red and furious when she opened the door. She looked down at Pella and turned to Snider Grant, who stood a few feet behind her.

"It's the Marsh girl," she said to her husband.

"Doug's not here," said Snider Grant angrily, without coming closer to the door.

"I know where Doug is," she said. "I want to see Morris."

"You ought to stay away from Doug," said Snider Grant, ignoring her, mashing his words gracelessly in his mouth. "He's bad trouble. He'll get *you* in trouble."

"Morris isn't here either," said Laney Grant. Her weary eyes flickered past Pella, into the dark valley, as if she feared Pella might be the advance scout for some ambush of the house.

"Neither of them stay here," said Snider. "Neither of them, anymore. I don't know where they go. Ask Efram Nugent."

"You haven't seen him?" said Pella.

"You heard him," said Laney. "They don't stay here." Morris appeared to be a bare afterthought to Doug, impossible to consider singly.

"Go on," grunted Snider Grant, turning away from the doorway. His wife nodded at Pella and closed the door.

Bruce Kincaid found her on the path back toward her house. He surprised her, coming out of the shadows. She felt her heart beating all the way to her fingertips, her toes, as she ran.

"What are you hiding for?" she said angrily.

"I snuck away," he said. "I had to talk to you."

"What?" Bruce couldn't help her with the thing she

needed to do. He didn't know about the Archbuilder in the shed, couldn't possibly be made to understand. He was from another life. His own urgent problems, whatever they were, only made her desperate with impatience.

"I was looking for you," he said. "I went to your house." He stood blinking at her there in the growing darkness, the time ticking away.

"Yes?" she said.

"What's the matter with your dad?"

"Nothing," she said, staring him down. She didn't want to think about Clement now.

"What's wrong with you?" she said.

"You heard about Martha."

"I heard something."

"My parents are packing up our stuff. We're going."

"Where?"

"Southport first. They're coming in the morning with a truck. But my dad's talking about Earth."

There is no town, thought Pella. There never was one. There had always only been Efram and whatever he wanted. A frontier, a prison, a fire.

The ones who might have made a town were gone, chased off or defeated, turned against one another, or themselves. Joe Kincaid. Ben Barth. Clement in his bedroom and Hiding Kneel in a shed, the useless ones, penned, made insane. Diana Eastling, gone. Now Ellen Kincaid and her bread. Pella hated Joe Kincaid now, as much as she'd ever hated anyone. Let him go. Let him protect his family and kill an Archbuilder on his way. Let him escape the Planet of Efram.

Pella wondered if she would ever know what really happened to Martha Kincaid.

"Are you crying?" said Bruce.

"No," said Pella.

"I might not see you again," he said.

"Do you want to stay?"

"Sure."

"Then don't go. Don't go back tonight." She surprised herself with the force of her yearning. Let her have Bruce here. He seemed precious now. That would be the cost of Joe Kincaid's going, the price for the Archbuilder in the shed.

Let her rob Joe Kincaid of his son. Let him know loss.

Bruce was silent, eyes lowered. Then, almost whispering, he said, "I can't, Pella. My family isn't like that."

Pella nodded.

"I should go back now," he said apologetically.

She understood that her family was like that, now. Hers and Morris's. So they would linger, while the Kincaids left. They would stay in the ruins. Families that weren't in a town that wasn't. Shame flooded her. And sadness.

She choked away the feeling, made herself hard again for what she had to do. As they stood together on the path the deepening night pooled around them. Soon it would be too dark. But Bruce could help her.

"I have to find Morris," she said.

"Why?"

"It's important," she said. "I can't explain. Where does he go at night?"

"I'll show you," said Bruce.

She followed him off the path, out past Wa's store, far into the valley. She watched him measure his direction by the jagged silhouettes that loomed on either side, making his last expedition, his silent farewell to the valley. A ghostly household deer whistled past them, into the dark. He guided her to the top of a ridge where a few distant lights were visible, Wa's, probably, and Bruce's own house. Then down again, through a twisting gorge, in absolute blackness. When they emerged into light again he took her hand.

"I should go," he said. "Morris is over there."

She squinted to see.

"You'll see his flashlight," said Bruce. "He has a hideout, kind of like yours. He calls it his clubhouse, but nobody's allowed except him."

He turned to her. She nodded. Then he released her hand and touched her shoulder, and leaned his head into hers, without closing his eyes. Their noses bumped, nestled together. She felt his lips touch hers, barely.

"Goodbye, Pella," he said. She could feel his breath on her face.

She moved closer and kissed him, catching his mouth with her own, holding it. He was dewy and soft.

They were both startled by it. Without meaning to, she thought of Efram, of standing with him in the empty valley an hour before. And then she thought of Doug Grant, and Hiding Kneel. Her breath skipped.

"Okay," she said, stepping back. She put her hand to her lips. This part of her was unfinished, lost. It couldn't be found now, not here.

A deer darted away.

Bruce turned back into the entrance of the gorge. In another moment he was swallowed in the gloom. She stood and watched him go, then went in the direction he'd pointed her, up a little rise. When she reached the top she saw the light, leaking out of the crevice at her feet.

She felt her way down off the rock and through the entrance to Morris's Archbuilder nook.

Morris was in the corner, lying on a blanket, reading his worn comic book by flashlight. He stared at her as she climbed in, his eyes wide and cowardly, his mouth sullen.

"I heard you and Bruce sneaking around," he said.

"Who cares?"

"You didn't surprise me. I knew you were coming."

Pella brushed the scuffs of dirt off her pants and knelt down on the corner of his blanket. "You knew I was coming because you were out there looking at us," she said. "As a deer." She only had to look for a moment to find it. Sitting on a crumbled shelf beside expired flashlight batteries and crusts of bread was an open jar of blue pills, perhaps twenty or thirty of them, with the blue sugar coating half smeared off by Morris's saliva. He'd pretended to take them, she knew, and hidden them under his tongue or in his cheek instead.

Morris watched her for a moment, then said, "So? I can if I want." Then, searching for an advantage, he said, "I saw you kissing."

She ignored it. "You sleep here now?"

"Sometimes," he said defiantly.

"Hiding Kneel comes here?"

"What?"

"You heard me. Hiding Kneel."

Morris stared at her again, and nodded. He was trembling.

She'd wound her way to the center. Outside the crevice where they huddled, night and silence covered the valley. Out there in the distance the Kincaids were packing their belongings, waiting for daylight, for their chance to escape, while others slept or lay awake, alone in various rooms, in ignorance, in loneliness, in distress. Outside Efram waited, ruling more than he knew. But here with Morris, in a hole lit by flashlight, Pella was at the core. She felt as cold and furious as a knife, one that would cut to the truth.

"You and Hiding Kneel spy on people together," said Pella. "You run around, outside. As deer."

"He made me," said Morris. "I swear. He taught me how."

"Hiding Kneel didn't make you stop taking the pills," she said. Morris just stared, still trembling. "What did you tell Doug?" she said.

"What?"

She crowded him in his corner, putting her face near his. His flashlight rolled away, its skewed light reeling across the floor. "What did you tell Doug? What did you make him think?"

"Nothing."

"Don't lie." Pella grabbed his hair. "You told him something about Hiding Kneel," she said. Flecks of her spit appeared on his face. She wanted to rub him in the dust. "About Martha and David. Tell me."

"I didn't lie," said Morris, his voice on the edge of panic. "It's true. Martha and David—"

"Martha and David what?"

"They were fooling around," said Morris, beginning to cry. "I saw her playing with his penis—"

"You were there as deer," said Pella. "Just like now, when you saw me kissing. You and Hiding Kneel were both deer. Martha and David don't know you saw them."

Morris started crying. "Don't hurt me."

"Doug doesn't know about household deer," said Pella. "You let him think you were really there. You and Hiding Kneel. You made him think you were all there together."

"He *asked* me—" Morris shrieked.

"You said what he wanted you to say," said Pella acidly. She let go of his hair. "Anything to make Doug happy. And Efram. Their sick minds. You're sick too."

"Martha and David—"

"Shut up. I don't care what they did. They're just kids."

"Hiding Kneel—"

"You killed him. You betrayed him."

She turned off his flashlight. The dark was apocalyptic. The two of them were only specks now, only voices. "I could kill you if I wanted."

Morris was less than a voice. He was a whimper. A fearful whine.

"No one would ever find your body," she whispered. "Bruce is gone, you know. His family is leaving."

Now he just wept.

Pella had her minuscule victory. She could undo Morris Grant. The bully whom everyone bullied she could bully too. His howling filled the darkness, filled the air.

"Don't kill me," he managed, between gasps for breath.

Pella reached out and found his wet, shocked face. He made a choking sound. She put her hand on his cheek, then his mouth, then his hair, feeling her anger evaporate as though seared by the heat of his face, turned to steam in the numbing, absolving darkness. In its place was shame, and exhaustion. She stroked Morris's hair, touched his ear and neck, wiped the mucus that soon stretched between her fingers onto the knee of her pants. His whimpering slowed. He still trembled. She crowded him again, but this time gently, with her shoulders. He fell against them, murmuring. She pulled the blanket up around him. He wheezed, sighed. She stroked his swollen eyelids.

Twenty

They walked together across the wastes, in the white blaze of the early sun. The sun had wrung the night out of the rocks; even in the shade it was too bright to look. They'd slept in their clothes, the boy and the girl, slept huddled cold in the dust under an inadequate blanket, but the whitish sun wrung the cold out of them too. The sun and their resoluteness. Very little had to be said. Their mouths were parched and crumbs remained in the corners of their eyes, but the girl was strong enough for both of them, and the boy was swept up, enclosed in her fierce resolve. They tracked past the vine-tangled ruins, past the house that had been converted to a shop, and then the girl led them a few steps out of their way, to look at the house of the family that was leaving. Early as it was, the family was already gone. The house empty. The girl stopped to examine the tire tracks on the ground and then without speaking she and the boy resumed their trek. Viewed from the sky, their path would have appeared as a straight line with a single dent, a line extending from the shard of ruin where they'd slept to the largest homestead in the valley.

"Hiding Kneel?"

There was a sound from inside the shed. The Archbuilder was still alive. Pella said, "Are you okay?"

Across from the shed, Doug Grant sat against Efram's greenhouse, head resting on his crossed arms, crossed arms resting on his upraised knees. Guarding the shed, protecting his prize, his captive. But fast asleep. A deer stood regarding him curiously. The waking valley was full of deer. The whole compound was silent, the scene bleached of the night's horrors.

"Only sleeping," said Hiding Kneel, in a dim voice. "I was dreaming of school—"

Then Morris tugged on her arm. "Pella."

It was Efram, coming out of his house. Pella saw only the line of his mouth as he strode toward them.

"Miss Marsh," he called out.

Pella stared back at him silently.

"Come to visit the prisoner?" he said once he stood only a few feet away, hands on hips, looming. "And you brought a friend this time."

Doug Grant lifted his head groggily at the boom of Efram's voice.

"Let Hiding Kneel out," said Pella. Her own voice sounded small, a squeak that could barely make its way out in the dead air. The dryness of her mouth and the heat of the morning seemed to erode the words before they crossed the space between her and Efram.

"You want to tell me why?"

"Because nothing happened," said Pella.

Doug Grant pulled himself up and moved toward them, blinking frantically in the sun, rubbing his legs as if they'd fallen numb. He stopped behind Efram.

"Get out of here, Morris," said Doug. "Go home."

"Morris lied to Doug, and Doug lied to you," said Pella to Efram.

She wanted Morris to speak, but he only stood beside her gaping idiotically at his brother and Efram.

She was alone. The men were gone—Joe Kincaid, Ben Barth, Clement. They were useless to her. The valley might as well have been empty. She stood alone facing Efram, with only Morris Grant to help her.

"Hiding Kneel didn't do anything to anybody," Pella went on, stringing together more of the dead, hopeless words. "Open the door," she said finally, making it as much a command as she could. She wanted it to be night again, she wanted to start a fire, do real damage. All she had were the words that died in the glare of day.

"Who put you in charge?" said Doug Grant, sneering. A minute before he'd been asleep. Now he vibrated with anger. He moved toward Pella, but Efram put his hand up and blocked him.

"Let her talk," said Efram, without looking at Doug. "She's got something on her mind."

"It's lies," she said again. "Morris lied. Tell him."

Morris blinked.

"Tell him," Pella said.

Morris hiccuped. "I didn't—"

"What are you talking about?" said Doug Grant. "You're crazy. She's *crazy*, Efram."

Efram didn't speak. He looked from Morris to Pella, and squinted under the shade of his hat.

"Doug doesn't know," Morris said, his voice wavering. "It happened different—"

"He's lying *now*, Efram," said Doug Grant shrilly. "She made him say it. I know what he told me. I know what I heard. And when Joe Kincaid asked Martha about it she started crying. His little *girl.*"

"Hiding Kneel didn't have anything to do with it," said Pella. "He didn't touch Martha, he wasn't even there. Doug doesn't know. Open the door."

Efram pursed his lips, moved just that much. Pella remembered the household deer he'd swept with such casual brutality from his path. Efram was moved that much now.

"You think I make my decisions based on what *Doug* tells me?" he said sardonically.

"What else do you know?" said Pella. "You weren't even around." Efram might be an edifice the words crashed against or a chasm into which they disappeared, but she could speak them now. "It was Doug and Joe Kincaid who stirred everything up. And Wa. What do you even know about it?"

"I know more than you or your little detective here. I know what I knew before you arrived on this planet, Pella Marsh."

"You don't know about Hiding Kneel. You just heard."

Now Efram smiled. "You of all people should know there's more than one way to learn things, Pella. What about Hugh Merrow?"

She looked at him appalled that he could even say that name aloud.

He was still abusing her secrets, still flaunting his crimes. Still flattering her. She felt warped by his monstrousness. She wanted to fall at his feet.

"Why think you're the only one around here who snuck a look at Merrow and his Archbuilder?" Efram went on.

Pella began to tremble. Did he inhabit household deer *himself*? Of course. Everything, anything. He lived in the rocks and the air.

Doug Grant stood openmouthed, baffled. The conversation had left him behind. The only thing certain was that his prize, his capture, was being taken from him one way or another. Efram had claimed it.

Meanwhile the disputed shed stood locked, the Archbuilder silent inside. They might as well have been arguing over freeing Ben Barth's chickens.

"You're a liar," Pella said. "And a killer." The words were unstoppable suddenly. If he didn't hear them she would plant them in the ground, and they would grow everywhere, like potatoes. "You killed Truth Renowned."

For a moment nobody spoke. Then Efram, his voice bitter, said, "Truth Renowned started a fire."

He didn't seem to be talking to Pella, only himself.

He took a step toward them, and Pella flinched. But it was Morris he reached for, with a flick of his hand that was lazy, indifferent. Morris twisted away and scurried behind Pella.

"Doug," said Efram, "take your brother home."

"The Archbuilder—" cried Doug, gesturing wildly. As though Hiding Kneel were about to burst out of the shack and terrorize the valley.

"*I'll* take care of the Archbuilder," said Efram impatiently. His voice was smoke. "And a few other things. Get your brother out of here. Leave me and Pella to talk."

"No," said Pella. She stepped backward and, not looking away from Efram, fished behind her until she found Morris's arm. She had her one weapon left. Fight spies with spies, she thought. Fires with fire.

Liars with lies.

"Say what you saw," she said to Morris, pushing him in front of her. "Say it now."

It seemed to Pella that it took Morris Grant an hour to produce the words, but in that time the four of them didn't move, and the air itself seemed impossibly still, frozen. They might not have been able to move through it if they'd tried. When he finally spoke the words they'd rehearsed together Morris was obnoxious, indignant, himself again for the first time since she'd made him weep in the darkened clubhouse the night before, as though for Morris it was only lies that inspired his truest self. And he was inspired. Brilliant.

"I saw *you!*" he shouted, pointing at Efram. "I saw you and Pella! I saw what you did!"

Nobody answered the cry. Nobody spoke.

"I saw you and Pella," said Morris again, his voice lowered insinuatingly now. "It was you."

Efram looked at Pella, narrowing his eyes. She met his gaze and nodded once. He understood. She would stand by the words. He knew the power in them. He should. Then she had to close her eyes, against the sun, against Efram. When she opened them he was only a throbbing black shape in the white glare.

"*Raper,*" said Morris. "*Fucker.*"

Efram stood staring at his hands. They were open, grasping slightly at nothing. Pella couldn't look at his face. She couldn't speak.

Doug Grant just stared at Efram, his eyes boiling with confusion.

"I told already," said Morris, his voice singsong, nagging. He'd surpassed the words he and Pella had planned together, was working off sheer inspiration now. "I told Wa, and Joe Kincaid. It's all over Southport by now. They'll get you."

Efram stood completely still now, though he beat like a pulse in Pella's vision.

"I told Diana Eastling you fucked Pella. I told everybody."

Lowering his head, Efram took a key from his pocket and went to the shed. He opened the padlock.

Then, in a movement so deft and sudden it was like a splash of water in the languid, spellbound morning, he reached out and grabbed Morris by the ear, and tugged him downward. Morris instantly buckled at the knees, cringing, whining. "Here's your Archbuilder, little brother," Efram said. "You deserve each other." Opening the shed, he shoved Morris inside, then forced the door shut and slipped the padlock back through the latch. In the instant the door was open Pella saw the Archbuilder sitting decorously in a corner on the floor, arms folded together, furred legs in a pool of fluid.

"Don't put him in there!" screamed Doug Grant.

Efram leaned his weight against the door lazily, and clapped the lock shut.

Doug Grant scrambled up from behind and pummeled on Efram's shoulders with his fists. "Let him out!" he screamed, his voice gone, shredded to a rasp. And from inside the shed, Morris screamed and beat on the door. It held.

Efram only had to shrug and Doug Grant was flung into the dust behind him, groaning.

"Pella," Efram said, not glancing back at Doug. "Inventive girl."

Pella stumbled backward. Morris howled inside the shed. Doug Grant dragged himself up, his face red and wet, and limped toward Efram's house. Efram took a step toward Pella. She turned, then tangled in her own legs and fell. She met the hard ground with palms, elbows, cheek. Her hands and face were stung. She tasted the grit. Like a deer watching dispassionately from a distant rock she saw her own skewed, half-finished self in misery on the hot ground. As Efram's shadow closed over her she shut her eyes in relief. Let him cover the sun. Let her go into the darkness. Efram could make the lie true if he wanted. She owed him that now. Who would miss her? Nobody. Clement was as dead as Caitlin. The rest were gone too. Brooklyn was forgotten. Pella was ready to finish her voyage to the Planet of the Archbuilders. She wouldn't miss herself.

She opened her eyes at the click. So she saw him a moment before he fired. In the bright sun he was another actor in black silhouette, his expression indistinguishable. He stood at Efram's house, pointing a rifle at Efram. His arms and the barrel of the rifle were shaking.

Efram turned his head away, as though he were barely interested. The shot exploded his chest.

Efram's arm reached up and swiped at the sky dismissively. He stumbled backward a step, two. Then he began to fall.

Doug Grant looked once into Pella's eyes, dropped the rifle, and ran, limbs flailing crazily, through the gate and out, across the rocks, into the unconquered distance.

Pella Marsh

David Marsh

Morris Grant

Llana Richmond

Julie Concorse

Melissa Richmond-

Concorse

Hiding Kneel

Lonely Dumptruck

Gelatinous Stand

Coral Dope

Truth Renowned

Unimportant Lust

Grinning Contrivance

Notable Beast

Specious Axiomatic

Somber Fluid

etc.

III

CAITLIN

Clement Marsh

E. G. Wa

Raymond Marsh

Snider and Laney Grant

Twenty-one

Hiding Kneel's chest had already healed somewhat. Under sodden fur shell had knit together in a thick crust, like an excess of glue squeezed out of a carpentered joint. A scar, or possibly a scab, something that would fall away. The Archbuilder moved slowly, tentatively, but it was alive. It was able to join the others in packing the upright figure with the black clay, though it didn't bend to scoop clay out of the bucket. Earlier it had only stood and watched as the other Archbuilders mounted Efram Nugent's body in the armature of wires and sticks.

Now Efram's corpse was nearly concealed inside the hardening sculpture. As the moisture evaporated, the figure turned the color of the valley floor, became another outcropping of the Planet. Another blunted shard pointing nowhere.

The three watching children moved off their vantage on the bluff and slipped away.

* * *

The flour was there in the kitchen, and the yeast. David collected eggs from Ben Barth's chickens while Morris dug up fresh cake and tea potatoes. Earlier that day she and David had moved their things out of Clement's house, into the Kincaids' empty rooms. Clement hadn't objected. David had barely even spoken, just latched onto Pella and followed her everywhere. Morris took a room too, marking it as his own by ceremoniously dropping his curled, greasy comic book on the floor. He'd been at Pella's side since the morning they felled Efram together.

Now Pella stacked charcoal in Ellen Kincaid's oven and arranged the bowls and pans, began measuring out scoops of flour.

Soon enough they were all kneading lumps of dough.

"Who's gonna buy it now?" said Morris. "Wa doesn't have any customers left."

"I don't know," admitted Pella.

"Archbuilders, maybe."

"Maybe."

Early in the morning Pella had felt the urge come back, and wandered out into the valley as a household deer. The pills didn't matter, once you knew how. The doors to Efram's were open, not just the house, but the greenhouse and Ben Barth's chicken coop, too. The chickens were still roosting inside, though. Freedom didn't tempt them. Pella-deer went inside the farmhouse. Archbuilders were sleeping in every available space, in the reconstructed Archbuilder room, in Efram's bedroom, in the kitchen. Hiding Kneel, Gelatinous Stand, Lonely Dumptruck, others Pella had never seen before. They'd moved in, the way she and Morris and David had moved into the Kincaids'.

None of what happened was really about Archbuilders, Pella decided. None of the humans had even met an Archbuilder, or even seen one. It was still all about the humans, what they saw when they looked at the Archbuilders, what they saw instead of the Archbuilders.

Maybe now they would meet them.

Maybe the Archbuilders would buy the bread.

"Morris said the Kincaids had to go because of what me and Martha did," said David.

He and Pella sat on the porch. Pella had traded the first batch of bread to Wa for cookies and soda and a brush and paint. The loaves were misshapen and heavy but Wa seemed grateful for the commerce, for the show of faith in the dwindled town. Now Pella worked on a hand-lettered sign, brushing white onto a plank rescued from Hugh Merrow's ruins. It read CAITLIN. Town of Caitlin, that would be the name. Because Caitlin brought them here. Not Clement, not really. Clement was as much a passenger as anyone.

Maybe the name would draw Raymond out of hiding, draw him back from Diana Eastling's house. Let the whole town be Raymond's mourning place. The lesbians, and Wa, and Diana Eastling if she ever came back—let them live in *Caitlin*.

Let poor sad crazy Clement live there too.

"Nobody made you do it, right?" she said.

"No."

"Then forget it. Joe Kincaid thought something else was going on. Something involving Archbuilders."

"We were just looking at each other. We didn't even—"

"Shut up about it. If nobody made you do it it's nothing to make a big deal about."

David started crying.

Be brave like an arm, Pella thought, but she didn't say it. Let David mother himself. Let him learn.

She searched the tattered horizon. Somewhere out there roamed Doug Grant. She was glad Bruce was gone now. She wasn't for him, not anymore if she'd ever been. After Caitlin it wasn't likely. There was something hard about her. Or worse than hard. Efram had made her, made her know herself, how far she'd traveled. It cost him, too.

She knew Doug Grant was the same. He'll come back, she thought. He'll grow up and come back, the new Efram. The one who doesn't fit in town. The one she killed was still alive in him.

That was who she would wait for.